THE LEGACY SERIES

SERIES TITLES

Never Stop Exiting
Michael Hopkins

Broken Heart Syndrome
Anne Colwell

The Mexican Messiah: A Novella & Stories
Jay Kauffmann

The Hopefuls
Elizabeth Oness

Close to a Flame
Colleen Alles

American Animism
Jamey Gallagher

Keeping What's Best Left Kept Secret
David Ricchiute

Soaked
Toby LeBlanc

The Path of Totality
Marie Zhuikov

Shocker in Gloomtown
Dan Libman

The Continental Divide
Bob Johnson

The Three Devils and Other Stories
William Luvaas

Maximum Speed
Kevin Clouther

Reach Her in This Light
Jane Curtis

The Spirit in My Shoes
John Michael Cummings

The Effects of Urban Renewal on Mid-Century America and Other Crime Stories
Jeff Esterholm

What Makes You Think You're Supposed to Feel Better
Jody Hobbs Hesler

Fugitive Daydreams
Leah McCormack

Hoist House: A Novella & Stories
Jenny Robertson

Finding the Bones: Stories & A Novella
Nikki Kallio

Self-Defense
Corey Mertes

Where Are Your People From?
James B. De Monte

Sometimes Creek
Steve Fox

The Plagues
Joe Baumann

The singular, wholly unpredictable stories collected in *Never Stop Exiting* prove once again that Hopkins is a writer with not only an unparalleled imagination, but an ear for the subtleties of language most of us never hear, an eye for the tiny details most of us would never notice, and an inherent understanding of the sometimes funny, sometimes frightened, sometimes merely confused human response to a world which, more often than not, can be really odd.

—JIM KNIPFEL
author of *Slackjaw*

In this bold and compelling collection, the quirky yet plentiful storytelling talent of Michael Hopkins covers an impressive range of milieus, offering masterful dialogue and surprises galore. As the founding fiction editor of *Coolest American Stories*, I can say without reservation that Michael's Coolest 2022 story "The Tallest Mountain in the World," which leads off this collection, will always be a favorite of mine. Read Michael Hopkins!

—MARK WISH
author of *Necessary Deeds*

The stories in *Never Stop Exiting* are simultaneously about a million random things—amputated legs, bee stings, Frank Zappa albums, Korean baseball players, a thrift store blazer, and so on—and about all the various kinds of loss and grief. The title is a revealing glimpse into the way humans slough off the dross of life and find meaning in what is left. Stealthily complex and persistently compassionate, Michael Hopkins's stories move like a curve ball: swerving, pivoting, and rising, to land in the reader's mitt with a satisfying grip.

—PHONG NGUYEN
author of *Bronze Drum*

These surprising stories start out in a variety of recognizable places and situations, and take you to places you never imagined you'd end up.

—ADAM LEVINE
editor of *Grow Magazine*

By delivering compelling characters, intriguing story-lines, and masterfully making connections between seemingly disparate elements, Michael Hopkins is not only a very fine short story writer, his work, I've found, can make you a more well-rounded human being. You'll emerge from your reading experience a more empathetic and intuitive individual. Lend your eyes to these tales and find out for yourself.

—JOHN BLONER, JR.,
Editor and Publisher, *Moss Piglet*

Michael Hopkins gives us gritty and real characters who navigate the ambiguity of change, seek to heal from the most painful of human experiences, or know exactly what they want and aren't afraid to say so. In both familiar settings and in near-futures, Hopkins's stories show us where grief, regret and loss may be transformed into possibilities and healing.

—NIKKI KALLIO
author of *Finding the Bones*

Existentialist moments inside a Chevy parked in a cornfield. An amputee demands her limb back. Torn toenails and dread. The murmurs of rivers, stones, and spores. The magnetic rhythm of Michael Hopkins' debut collection combines snappy prose with meditative narrative that draws you into worlds that are a circle that somehow has an extra edge. An edge from which you look up and realize it's well after midnight. Savor these stories now, feel them linger for days.

—STEVE FOX
author *Sometimes Creek*
Rick Bass Montana Prize Winner

The stories in this collection are honest, funny, warm, and compelling. Some move through you like a freight train, some like a prayer, but they all make you reflect on the vastness of the human experience as it plays out in the lives of ordinary people doing ordinary things. The characters in the stories are so richly composed, that it's like watching De Niro and Streep at the top of their game. Hopkins's writing is charming, sarcastic, and keen, and through the stories, you will fall in love with humanity!

—JUDY BAUERLEIN
Professor of Theater
California State University, San Marcos
Director of *Static*

NEVER STOP EXITING

STORIES

MICHAEL HOPKINS

CORNERSTONE PRESS

UNIVERSITY OF WISCONSIN-STEVENS POINT

Cornerstone Press, Stevens Point, Wisconsin 54481
Copyright © 2025 Michael Hopkins
www.uwsp.edu/cornerstone

Printed in the United States of America by
Point Print and Design Studio, Stevens Point, Wisconsin

Library of Congress Control Number: 2025934208
ISBN: 978-1-960329-83-7

Cornerstone Press titles are produced in courses and internships offered by the Department of English at the University of Wisconsin–Stevens Point.

DIRECTOR & PUBLISHER
Dr. Ross K. Tangedal

EXECUTIVE EDITORS
Jeff Snowbarger, Freesia McKee

EDITORIAL DIRECTOR
Brett Hill

SENIOR EDITOR
Ellie Atkinson

PRESS STAFF
Cora Bender, Andrew Glazer, Karlie Harpold, Eliot Javers, Lillian Kulbeck, Emma Meronek, Anthony Thiel, Holly White, Sophie McPherson, Madison Schultz, Autumn Vine, Ava Willett

For Heidi

The Tallest Mountain
in the World

Dr. Merton gave Shelby Aronowitz bad news. The pain in her knee was osteosarcoma. They would have to amputate the leg.

"Can't they replace it?" Shelby's mother asked. "Just the knee, I mean?"

"No," Dr. Merton said. "We need to remove bone too far above and below the joint." He brought up an image from Shelby's MRI. On the large screen in the small room, he pointed at the dark spots. He cleared his throat. "But the good news is you can be fitted with a prosthetic leg. The technology is evolving quickly. There's no reason you can't have a full life."

Shelby's mother wrapped her arms around Shelby's broad shoulders and began to cry. It wasn't her strongest embrace. Shelby pictured her mother on a typical day, in bed at noon, propped up with pillows, a box of Kleenex on her lap, whining on the phone to Aunt Arella about this or that.

Dr. Merton continued, "Ride a bike, dance, even run. You have a very strong physique."

Shelby pulled away from her mother and stretched out her leg. "I want to keep it," she said.

No one answered her, so she glanced up at Dr. Merton's face. It reminded her of the fudge cheese her Aunt Arella made and sometimes gave her: chew it all you want but you could taste neither fudge nor cheese.

He finally spoke up to say, "Not recommended. It's localized now, but probably, very likely, it will spread into some of your other systems."

"No," Shelby said. "What I'm saying is—all I'm saying is, I want to keep the leg."

"Shelby," her mother said. "For God's sake, listen to the man. He knows what he's talking about."

"You don't know what *I'm* talking about," Shelby said. "I want to keep what they cut off." She stood and remained standing despite the pain shooting from her knee up into her groin.

"Impossible," her mother said. "Right, Doctor? Tell her."

Dr. Merton looked at his watch and stood. Obviously he had other patients to see, some with cancer, some without.

He turned to Shelby's mother. "Believe it or not Mrs. Aronowitz…believe it or not , there *is* a protocol for Shelby's request." He allowed himself to take in a deep breath. "As a minor, she'd need your approval, and there'd be plenty of papers for you to sign, and a few additional costs, but, to be honest with you, it's not impossible."

"No way," Shelby's mother said. "No way are we spending money to be reminded of how you had cancer."

"Says who?" Shelby asked.

"Says me," her mother replied. "Who else?"

THE PHONE RANG and Shelby's mother answered it and put it on speaker and set it beside her on her bed, as she was wont to do. Shelby, in her own room, wasn't listening closely at first, even though she recognized the voice as belonging to her Uncle Jacob. Then, after she heard her name mentioned, she tiptoed over to the slightly open door to her room, opened it wider, gave their conversation her full attention.

"No, listen to me," her Uncle Jacob was saying. "You should know something. I talked to her. She wants me to sue you."

"Sue me? Did you say sue me?"

"Yes."

"But I'm her mother."

"She also told me the cancer has changed her. No more aspiring to be an actress; she wants to go into law."

Shelby's mother went silent.

"Can't you imagine," Uncle Jacob said, "Shelby and my little Zeke, seeing to it that the family business lives on? Benjamin and I discussed this many times when he was alive. And Shelby would be a great attorney, by the way. My brother—I mean, your husband—is now doubtless smiling down on how well this could all turn out."

Shelby's mother was still at a loss for words.

Then: "You are *not* seriously considering this."

"*Aronowitz and Aronowitz.* I thought it would end when Benjamin passed, but now it could live forever. There's that psalm Benji loved so much: 'One generation shall commend your works to another, and shall declare your mighty acts.'"

"You're saying this psalm was written for Shelby's ears?"

"I'm saying it was written and her father read it and said it out loud many times, and I'm sure she heard it—because, well, even though he's gone now, here we are."

"Well, if the point of her practicing law is so she can sue her mother, I'm not sure the psalm ended up doing what it was supposed to."

"That's not the point of her wanting to practice. They're two separate things, her wanting to practice and her wanting to sue you by having me file a complaint."

"So you're telling me you're going to let her do it."

"Do what?"

"Sue her own mother."

"Of course we're not going to let her sue you," he said. "Because she has a case, which means you *really* don't want her to sue you. This is why I called you. I agreed to work with her, and she's my deceased brother's daughter, so now I'm letting you know you should stop trying to control what she and I and for that matter God will succeed in doing anyway."

"What do you mean, work with her?"

"I've researched it. There's no law here against keeping the leg, or any body part. In some states—Louisiana, Georgia, Missouri, it's against the law—but even there, if you're part of certain religious groups that believe the body is physically resurrected, as when Christ supposedly returns, you can keep these parts to be buried with you."

Shelby smiled. Her uncle, she realized, was as full of subtle wit as he was smart.

"Jacob, do you hear yourself?" her mother asked.

"Even in states where there is no law against this…I have it right here. The *Native American Graves Protection and Reparation Act* makes it illegal to own or trade in Native American remains. It's unclear to me if this still applies to Native American individuals and their own body parts. But see, that's not our problem here."

"Can we quit discussing this?" Shelby's mother asked, and Shelby, holding on to the doorframe because her knee was throbbing, rolled her eyes.

"Sure, but you should probably know a reporter's already been here," Jacob said. "From *The Sentinel*."

"About Shelby?"

"Not at first," Jacob said. "He wanted to interview me about the Brazilian acquisition of *Madison Dynamics*. This reporter was a young man, but nice. I couldn't answer most of his questions for legal reasons, but then Shelby called— right then, right when he was sitting across my desk. And

I was so happy about her decision to go into law, I told this young man everything she told me."

Jacob paused long enough that Shelby was sure her mother would go off. But all Shelby heard was the sound of herself breathing.

"I thought the leg thing might have been a joke," Jacob continued, "since Benjamin was always a practical joker. I never knew when to believe him and figured maybe it had rubbed off on her. Anyway, this reporter plans to talk to her. I guess her leg is news."

"My God, Jacob."

"I may have made an error in judgment," Jacob said. "That's basically why I called you."

"My God."

"You've got Benjamin's ashes on the mantle in your living room. I don't see harm in letting Shelby hang her leg on the wall of her bedroom. Seriously, what would be the harm?"

The call ended, apparently because Shelby's mother hung up. For the first time, Shelby imagined her bad leg mounted on the wall above her bed. It would be visible from the street at night if she had the light on and the shades up, she realized.

And she thought, No.

Not there.

Someplace else.

DESPITE HAVING VERY LITTLE factual information, the reporter's article ran the following Sunday, in the community section of *The Sentinel*.

Upon reading it, Shelby's mother said, "I want you to sue *them*."

"There's nothing slanderous or fallacious in the article," Uncle Jacob said. He was visiting, drinking coffee with Shelby and her mother that morning. "We have no legal grounds."

"But the thing is, she's being taunted at school."

"I'll be fine, Mother," Shelby said, sipping coffee.

But Shelby's mother pressed on, facing Jacob: "At dinner she tells me a boy, a hunter, offered to mount her leg. And now we're getting calls from other reporters, the TV wants her to come in and be interviewed *live and on the air.* I'm losing my mind!"

"Why?" Jacob asked her. "So they ask a few questions? She answers them and—"

"You were going to sue me," Shelby's mother said. "All I'm saying is I want you to sue *them*—to get them to stop."

"That might backfire," Jacob said. "I mean, they might write articles about *that.* I say just sign the consent form. She needs surgery and wants the leg. You're holding her back."

Shelby's mother fretted, then frowned. She batted her eyes angrily.

"This is an abomination," she said.

SHELBY SAT ON THE EDGE of her bed and straightened out both legs. She thought the right one, the cancer leg, was a little shorter than the left. Certainly that knee hurt more than it had the day before. Her phone rang, caller unidentified. She answered it with a flat "Hello?"

"Am I speaking with Shelby Aronowitz?" The caller had one of those low-toned voices, a late-night radio voice.

"Yes," Shelby said. "Who's this?" She settled back and shut her eyes, and her shoulders dropped, a puppet with the strings cut.

"Glen Smith," the caller said. "I work for—actually, I own—Casselton Skulls. We specialize in the preservation and sale of bones: mostly skulls, animal skulls, and some full skeletons."

Shelby sat up. "Is this a joke?" She tried to place the voice. "Who is this? How did you get my number?"

"Please, Miss Aronowitz, this is not a crank call. We are one of two companies in the States that handle human needs of your type."

Shelby thought he now sounded like the man from the funeral parlor who'd met with her mother and her after her father died. There'd been an attempt at solemnity in that man's tone, and Shelby had known right away back then that this must be part of the job, so with this guy, this Glen Smith guy, she wanted to believe that he was genuine—that he understood and cared, but she had her doubts about that.

"When you say my needs," she managed to say, "what do you mean exactly?"

"I would receive your leg, personally and directly, from the surgeon. In advance I would discuss his methodology with him to ensure the separation from the body is done…with respect, I mean with more care than is taken by surgeons who tend to be in a hurry. If you wish, I could even offer to be present at the procedure."

Shelby realized she hadn't thought through the details of what happened between the surgery and when she'd be handed back her leg.

"You've done this before?" she asked.

"Yes. We don't deal with soft tissue: breasts, ovaries, intestinal lengths, or tumors. Just bones—kneecaps, feet, hands. But we've never had the privilege of such a large portion of a limb. You'd be our first."

"How much does this cost?"

"It might seem insensitive to charge you, but not charging you would set a precedent—everyone would expect the same. Though we *are* prepared to give you a 30% discount, meaning our fee of $3,000 would be reduced to $2,100. And, should you want one, we'd provide an extra observer at the procedure for no charge."

"Why so much money?" Shelby wanted to know. "My friend had a deer head mounted for four hundred bucks."

"Here's our process: after removal and transportation, we deflesh the limb with Dermestid beetles, a very common practice in this industry, and then, of course, we sterilize and whiten the bones."

"So I'd get only the bones."

"Correct. But they'd be spotless and disinfected."

"May I ask what you do with the beetles when they're done?"

"After skeletonization is complete, we keep half and any associated larvae; the other half we release back into nature."

"Could I choose where the beetles are released?"

"We've never had that request, but I'm sure we could work it out."

Shelby imagined a package arriving by an overnight Federal Express. Inside would be part of herself, solid and clean and permanent.

"Well, I'm interested," she said to Glen Smith.

"You'll also be glad to know we wire the bones together to ensure long-term stability. In your case we'd be dealing with quite a few bones: four in the knee, fourteen in the ankle, and thirty-eight in the foot. Labor intensive. I'm assuming you want the leg intact, versus a box of bones, which we could do at a greatly reduced rate."

"Oh, no," Shelby said. "I mean you're right—if I'd do this with you, I'd want the leg in one piece."

"Very good, Miss Aronowitz. We would suggest that."

"The thing is, I need to talk to my mother about the money."

"We've handled that for you. Have you heard of the Mutter Museum, in Philadelphia?"

"No."

"They have a large and varied collection of human artifacts. About three thousand. Wet and dry."

Shelby wondered how they distinguished between wet and dry. Was it how the piece arrived in their hands, or how it was displayed?

"They have parts of Einstein's brain and John Wilkes Booth's spine."

Glen Smith paused. He seemed to want a "wow" from Shelby, but she remained quiet as she tried to figure out where he was going with all this.

Then he said, "They've offered to pick up the cost if you agree to will them your leg, to be delivered after you…pass on, which, naturally, we're all hoping won't be for a long, long time."

"Why would they want to do that?" Shelby asked. "I'm not famous."

"Uh…if Twitter is any indication, your fame will be growing for quite a while."

"Really? I'm not a Twitter person—"

"Hashtag *Keeping It*. Everyone's into you, Shelby, and most of them think you're pretty cool. And they seem to enjoy exchanging theories about why you want to do this."

Shelby was taken aback. Twitter? She'd always been more into Instagram, where she'd posted nothing whatsoever about her leg.

Why Twitter? she wondered. Did that reporter tweet something?

"Do you mind," Glen Smith asked, "if I ask you?"

"Ask me what?"

"Why you want to keep it?"

"I'm not sure," Shelby said.

"I'm guessing the answer is part of the same mystery we've dealt with again and again. It's a feeling, a calling, a notion that something—some action that's out of the ordinary—is significant."

"Yes," Shelby said. "That's a good way of putting it. What you're talking about right there—that feeling—that's pretty much the feeling I've felt."

SHELBY SAT AT THE TABLE in front of a plate of wild-caught salmon and broccoli florets, Googling images of Glen Smith: buzz cut, a plain face pink as a pencil eraser, a fairly honest-looking guy.

Her mother finished her dinner quickly and started washing the dishes. For almost forty minutes, neither she nor Shelby spoke.

Shelby broke the unspoken truce:

"Mom. No charge. A guy named Glen Smith at a place called Casselton Skulls does this with human bones full-time."

A plate fell from her mother's hand and smashed on the kitchen floor. Pieces shot everywhere. Thankfully this plate wasn't from the good china in the front room cabinet; this was an everyday plate. Still, there was redness in Shelby's mother's cheeks. The redness of embarrassment the redness of rancor, the redness of both—Shelby couldn't be sure.

"Fuck all these people!" her mother shouted. "Fuck all these reporters, fuck your uncle, fuck my friends! Who *is* this guy who wants to petrify your leg? You. Are. *Dying*, Shelby! You need *cancer surgery!* First your father, and now I'm also supposed to lose *you?* Fuck your leg—I don't ever want to see it again. Fuck everybody. Fuck you!"

She grabbed a wet glass from the sink and pitched it at the floor, Shelby shielding her eyes from ricocheting shards.

Shelby feared for her life as another glass shattered.

Then another, and another, and another.

"YOU'LL SEE A COUNSELOR," Shelby's mother said.

She was standing just beyond the open door to Shelby's room.

"You'll see a counselor," she added, "if you want any chance whatsoever at having me sign those papers."

"*I'll* see a counselor?" Shelby asked from her bed, phone in hand.

Her mother nodded.

"*You'll* see a counselor," Shelby said. "That is, if you want any chance at having me have the surgery in the first place."

"Oh, don't going playing insolent."

"I'm not, Mom. All I'm doing is letting you know that you have as many problems as I do."

Shelby's mother raised her before-dinner wine to her lips, sipped some, and said, "Okay, but only if you see the guy, too."

"You mean go with you?" Shelby asked.

Her mother sipped again, this time maybe less out of habit.

"No," she said. "I mean we'd go separately. I want us both to be able to tell the truth."

"Okay," Shelby said, the pain in her leg all at once worse, and her mother turned around and walked off without a sound.

And Shelby's mother stayed that way—silent—for the three days that passed before Shelby was off, out of the house, driving their only car herself despite her bad leg, which she'd told her mother felt fine but didn't, to see Dr. Lubitsch.

Dr. Lubitsch's office itself was large. Dark. Slatted wooden shades covered the windows. Floor to ceiling bookshelves lined the walls, crammed with sets of old hardbacks. Shelby kept her eyes on the books as she walked to the brown leather chair Dr. Lubitsch had motioned her to sit in. She could not recognize a single title. She thought the lights in the room needed brighter bulbs. How could the guy read in here? She sank into the chair. The chair enveloped her, was comfortable.

"Nice to meet you, Shelby," Dr. Lubitsch said. He sat on a straight-backed chair across the room.

Shelby nodded in his direction.

"Are you comfortable?" he asked. "How does your knee feel?"

"It hurts. Like a bad sprain that won't get better."

"Yes," Dr. Lubitsch said. "And I understand it won't."

Shelby winced. It was as if this man was about to recite lines her mother had emailed him.

"Still holding out hope?" he asked. "For a miracle?"

Shelby shrugged.

"That's normal," Dr. Lubitsch said. "I've seen many patients who hope for miracles, but I've never seen a miracle that can't be explained." He shifted in his chair. "There *are* solutions, though, based on science. The mind can work wonders. It can be tuned to work better than it normally does."

Shelby laughed a nervous beat's worth. "So what are you saying? What are you saying my problem is?" She was anxious to talk about her mother. About how she'd had to do everything for her mother the first year after her father's death: the cleaning, the cooking, always making sure her mother took her meds. About how her mother never let her use the car, going as far as hiding the keys. About how she'd then always wondered if her mother would be there to pick her up after school activities—about having to hitchhike home more than once. How her mother would then, on those nights, refuse to make eye contact, never listening about how *Shelby* felt about the man who, yes, had been her mother's spouse, but who had also been Shelby's father. How her mother never paid much attention to her until now.

Dr. Lubitsch finally composed himself enough to say quietly, "I never said you had a problem." He was a small man, perfectly proportioned but very small. "We're here to talk—that's it."

Shelby rolled her eyes. The deck was clearly stacked against her with this jerk. She tipped back her head and looked at the top of a bookshelf, on which sat skulls. Some were big, one maybe from a massive boar; another obviously from a horse's head. Many with horns both straight and curved. Some tiny ones, probably from birds.

Dr. Lubitsch turned in his chair. "Do those bother you?"

"No," Shelby said. "I like them."

"Some of my patients don't," he said. "I usually meet clients in a different room. I was wondering if you'd appreciate them."

"I do," Shelby said. "When did you start collecting them?"

"The first was the horse skull I found in the trash. I trash-pick around the university when the students move out. You can find lots of interesting stuff. I didn't really have a collection until people—friends, clients, so forth—started giving me skulls they'd come across. The coyote is from Colorado, from a woman suffering from a borderline personality disorder. The ram is from Nevada. That particular young man had bipolar tendencies. The large bird was from an elderly couple I treated for hoarding; their collection is vast compared to mine. The deer was from a friend, a hunter who also likes to give me venison every year."

He scanned the collection, his eyes stopping here and there.

"Each has a story."

"I imagine," Shelby said.

"Did you know," Dr. Lubitsch asked, "that some forms of meditation direct you to imagine your flesh dropping away until you're just a skeleton? Then you're supposed to imagine removing your head—as just a skull now, of course—from your body, and inserting it, upside down and reversed, under your ribcage."

He patted his stomach as if maybe Shelby hadn't understood.

"I've heard it's quite effective," he added.

Whatever, Shelby thought, but she said, "I don't see why it wouldn't be."

"Do you know what phantom limb pain is, Shelby?"

Shelby nodded. "I've read about it."

"Sometimes patients go out of their minds with the pain, believing that their lost limb is spasming." He held out his hand and made a fist. "Clenching up."

"Isn't there medication for that?"

"No. Acupuncture, massage, the mirror box. Have you heard of that?"

Shelby shook her head no.

"Let's say you've lost your right arm. Imagine you are sitting to the side of a big mirror, and you insert your stump into a box behind the mirror. You are then instructed to look at the reflection of your other arm and imagine it's the one that's missing." He held both his arms out. "When you stretch out your good arm and wiggle your fingers, you look at the reflection and imagine it's your other arm, the missing one."

Shelby nodded, trying to remain patient until they talked about her mother.

"You don't seem too impressed," Dr. Lubitsch said.

"Sounds like something that could work just fine for some people. For me, I think simply keeping my leg will help me be cool with what's what."

Dr. Lubitsch nodded slowly a few times. His eyes seemed to twinkle just a bit for a few moments on end. Or maybe, Shelby, thought, I'm imagining that. She looked back up, at the top of the bookshelf with the skulls.

She pointed. "Is that from a cat?"

"Yes," Dr. Lubitsch said, looking up as well. "My Smokey. Had him thirteen years, then…well, I hate to say this, but cancer got him."

Shelby waited for his gaze to meet hers, then brightened her expression as if to say, *See?*

"Sometimes I hold his skull," Dr. Lubitsch admitted. "I wonder if the seat of the soul isn't in the skull." He smiled. "Once a friend wanted to give me a human skull, but my wife said no. Too creepy." He glanced at Shelby's bad leg.

She pointed again. "What's that one? Where did you get it?"

Dr. Lubitsch looked up at the large, damaged skull. "A long story." He leaned in. "It's fragments of an Allosaurus."

"How old is it?"

"About 150 million years."

"Immortal," Shelby said. "In a way."

Dr. Lubitsch raised his eyebrows.

Then he nodded.

"Shall we talk about your mother?" he asked.

"Sure."

"Tell me what's your biggest gripe concerning her."

"That she's not talking to me. Hasn't been for days. And that, last we spoke, she made it clear she still doesn't want to sign the papers that would let me keep my leg."

DURING THE NEXT TWO WEEKS, Shelby became nervous about everything. It didn't help that the day after she met with Dr. Lubitsch, she met with two young doctors, one who would be her surgeon. They were both very direct, even more so than Dr. Merton had been about the fact that she would be "knocked out" for the surgery. About the need to "amputate." These were the words they used, "knocked out" and "amputate," as well as other turns of phrase that assured her and anyone else within earshot that they were, probably because of their training, all business. As she met with them, she felt herself shift into a new level of nervousness, which she tried to convince herself was normal.

Then, during the nearly two weeks that followed, as she waited for the day of the surgery itself, she found herself feeling this level of nervousness about everything. It was hitting her, the significance of the changes that were coming to her life. For most of the twelve hours before her surgery she sat in her room where she was waited on by her mother, who told her again and again to remain immobile, a directive one of the young, no-nonsense doctors, the one who was not the surgeon, had given her mother over the phone.

Her mother said little else to her, certainly nothing about signing the papers that would let her keep her leg, and at first this reticence disappointed Shelby, but, as the twelve days went on, Shelby sensed courage was not her mother's greatest strength, and she felt sorry for her mother and tried to please her by keeping their conversations as short as possible.

It was with six days to go summer break started. A bad coincidence of timing, since this only reminded Shelby she was not outside running or walking or doing whatever every other person her age was doing, now that the weather was nice and school wasn't weighing anyone down. For her it was now only Google this, Google that, eat, watch a Netflix movie, check Instagram, check Facebook, binge a TV series, eat, check Insta, sleep, wake up, check Facebook to allow more possibly interesting posts to build up on Insta when she'd finally break down to allow herself to click up Insta again.

It was during these last six days that she realized she didn't have any real friends.

At least none that were real enough to stop by and visit.

Her Uncle Jacob and Aunt Arella had been stopping by sometimes during the last six days, maybe three or four times altogether—but family doesn't count as friends.

THEY WERE SITTING on two leather chairs in Shelby's father's old study. Shelby was glad to be out of her bedroom, finally allowed to move around, and she didn't mind talking to Dr. Lubitsch. Her mother came in and gave them each a glass of coconut-flavored sparkling water. Her mother left and pulled the door shut until the latch clicked.

"Were you always active at school?" Dr. Lubitsch asked.

"After my father died."

Shelby squeezed the thigh of her bad leg and scanned the room. Her father's old, dirty coffee mug sat on his desk, adjacent to the last legal pad he'd used, his cartridge ink pen still lying on top. The blinds were down. It was quiet.

Shelby said, "I did a lot more with my father than I knew, until I really thought about it. Fishing. Hiking. Talking. Once we drove clear around a lake, like a hundred miles on a Sunday afternoon, just to do it."

Dr. Lubitsch, appearing more comfortable here than in his own office, said, "You could be…over-functioning, a lot of activity with no meaningful connections. A behavior not uncommon when filling a void. Never a minute to stop and take a breath. Like an insect, a water strider, zigzagging on the top of life's pond, afraid to stop for fear of sinking. Our technology, all the screens we carry, makes it easy."

Shelby wanted to check her phone, felt guilty, and instead reached into her pocket and just touched it.

Dr. Lubitsch leaned back. "And your mother?"

"What about her?"

"Has she decided whether to sign the papers?"

"I thought that's what you were going to tell me."

Dr. Lubitsch shrugged.

"I guess she's still deciding," he said. "But I guess that's her right. It's a big decision for both of you, you know."

No, it's not, Shelby wanted to say. It's a big decision for me, and it's not right that she's not letting me make it.

"Anyway," Dr. Lubitsch said. "How are you two getting along of late?"

"I'm mean to her. Probably more than I should be."

"Not uncommon for teenagers. Especially if the opposite sex parent with whom you had a good relationship is now gone." Dr. Lubitsch waited to see if this registered with Shelby. "Very common in divorce."

Shelby swirled her drink. Bubbles in it rose to the surface and fizzed. It was a comforting sound for Shelby, and it reminded her of the time when she was maybe three or four, when her father bundled her up to take her on an adventure. They drove through a blizzard to a golf course and hiked to the ninth hole. Looking down, Shelby thought they were on the tallest mountain in the world. Her father positioned the red plastic toboggan with him in the back and Shelby in the front, secured between his legs, then launched them with three strong pushes. The world rushed by. Snow stung her face and she screamed in delight. At the bottom, they turned and tumbled off into a drift. They laughed. For a moment before they got up, her father squeezed her in his wiry but strong arms, kissed the top of her head. He told her to shut her eyes and listen, listen to the sound of the falling snow. And she did. She heard it come at her from all directions.

"Shelby?" Dr. Lubitsch said.

Shelby looked up from her glass. Scanned the room and this time saw the urn.

"Once, when we were hiking," she said, "my dad told me he wanted to be buried in a forest, in a biodegradable coffin that would let his body decompose into the ground. So he could live on as part of the trees."

"I've heard of that method," Dr. Lubitsch said. "Honorable."

"Since then, I always imagined walking through the woods, alone, or with my own children someday. Feeling his presence."

"Where is he now, Shelby? Do you ever think about that?"

Shelby bit her thumbnail and pointed with her head. "Right up there." She talked around her thumb. "My mother had that done."

"Did she know about your father's wishes?"

Shelby pursed her lips, then said, "I think so. I mean *yes*."

THE OPERATING ROOM was nothing like Shelby had imagined: small, low ceiling, mostly beige and gray, hardly any equipment. Each member of the team was busy with a task. A nurse inspected neatly lined up instruments. A doctor watched a screen, another positioned a camera over her leg. Another nurse swabbed her knee with something cold.

Dr. Merton stood over Shelby. He was there to assist and observe. He had a mask on so she could not see his face below his eyes. One of his eyes was bloodshot.

"We're going to give you something to help you relax," he said, and Shelby watched the nurse put a needle into the IV port burrowed into her arm. She barely felt the sting, she felt nothing until she woke up, when she heard incessant, calm beeps keeping track of something, her heart, she hoped.

She opened her eyes. A nurse probably near retirement was covering her up to her waist with a thin blanket. She didn't remember why she was here until she remembered the cancer and looked down toward her leg.

It was gone, clearly. Gone. But she was still breathing and her heart was still beating, if faster. And the other leg was still there, and her arms were still there. She raised the arm that wasn't hooked up to things to see if it could move, and it could, as could her good leg.

"You're up," the nurse said. "You'll feel groggy for a while. Is there anything I can get you?"

Shelby could think of nothing except her father.

"Maybe some water?" the nurse asked. "Some ice chips?"

"Is my mother here?" Shelby asked.

"I believe so," the nurse said. "At least she was a few minutes ago."

"Could you please get her?"

"Sure. But then that's all you want for now? Maybe a cracker—"

"Yes, please. Just her."

The nurse nodded and walked off as if Shelby had all the power in the world.

The beeps beeped. Shelby waited.

The door to the room swung open, and her mother walked in, followed by Uncle Jacob, followed by Aunt Arella, followed by Glen Smith, who was straining somewhat to carry the long, white plastic bag he was hugging against his chest.

"Mom," Shelby said as her mother stopped beside the bed, even as Glen Smith kept walking all the way in, so he could hand Shelby the white bag, inside which she could feel her leg, which had not yet gone completely cold.

And Shelby's mother said, "*Shelby.*"

Static

I got stung. Three bees were on my ankle; I could feel them right through my sock. I brushed them off, escaped from our vegetable garden where I was weeding, and ran into the house.

"Damn it," I said to Betty, my wife, who was chopping carrots, "I got stung."

"Where?" Betty asked. "On your face again?"

"My ankle." I pulled down my sock and showed her the marks. Three red dots were already starting to swell.

"Right now, take some Benadryl," she said.

"I'll be fine."

"You always say that," she said. "Your ankle is going to blow up like a balloon, and you'll be up all night." She turned to our kitchen cabinet. "Here it is." She dumped the pink pills into her palm, picked two, and gave them to me. "Take 'em."

I got some water and swallowed the pills. When I was younger, bee stings never bothered me, but, as I got older, my reaction was worse and worse. I'm not sure why. As a kid, I prided myself for never getting poison ivy, or fevers, or allergies, or needing glasses—the commonplace weaknesses among my friends. Perhaps I missed some physical inflection point in my life. I've been so busy, I'm sure I've missed a lot of things.

My dad came into the kitchen. "What happened?"

My wife pointed to my foot, which had started to swell. "Gary got stung in the garden."

"Put mud on it," my dad said. "It draws out the poison."

"Listen to your father." She nodded. "Mud will help."

"I'll get some dirt," my dad said.

"Don't go near the garden," my wife said. "That's where the bees are."

He nodded. "I'll steer clear of them."

We ate a late dinner together around the kitchen table. My foot, covered in mud, and resting on a towel, was propped up on a spare chair.

"I think we should call an exterminator," my wife said.

"I'll take care of it," I said. My foot had started to itch.

"This is the third time you got stung this month." My wife put a forkful of kale into her mouth. "When?"

"Tonight," I said. "I know what to do. It's a ground hive. We just need to pour ammonia into the hole, at night, when the bees are dormant."

"Not ammonia," my dad said. "Gasoline."

"Are you nuts," I said, "that would be dangerous."

"Well," he said, "don't the terrorists use ammonia to make bombs? That might be more dangerous." My father sipped his iced tea. "Did you hear about that attack in Paris? I saw it on the news. What's wrong with these people that they would blow themselves up?" He straightened in his chair. "Before long they're going to start doing it over here."

"Let's not start in on this again," my wife said. "Can't we have a normal conversation at dinner for once? No politics." My wife dropped her fork on the plate and glared at me.

"I'll do it tonight," I said.

My dad looked under the table. "What's with your foot?"

MY WIFE AND I WERE IN BED. I'd finished revising a presentation I was on deck to present the next day. I looked at my foot. It appeared stable. The drugs and mud had done the job. My wife was turned on her side, asleep, and I turned off my light.

"We need to talk," my wife said in the darkness. She sat up and turned on her nightstand lamp. "We need to do something."

"I poured a gallon of ammonia into the hole," I said. "They should all be dead by morning."

"You know that's not what I'm talking about."

"Listen," I said, "I'm tired. My foot hurts. I don't want to argue. Can we just go to sleep?"

"No, we can't. We have to move your father."

I turned on my light. "Let's give the in-home care another try."

"No," she said. "We tried that twice, and they both quit after a few days." She raised her hands in the air. "He threw a cup of coffee at the last one."

"She was messing with his maps."

"That's another thing." my wife said. "His crap is spread out all over the living room: maps, fishing gear, his lure projects." She turned to me and rubbed my shoulder. "You love your father. I do, too. But it's been three years, and he's getting worse. More than we can handle."

"I'll work with him to keep the living room clean."

"It's not just that," my wife said. "TJ found him wandering on his property the other day. And I came home from work yesterday, and your father had emptied all the kitchen drawers. He said he was looking for the car keys so he could pick up your mother."

"Maybe my brother…"

"Your brother won't be of any help, and you know it. We're in this alone." She waited for me to respond. "We haven't been able to take a proper vacation for three years."

"We haven't done a lot of things in three years."

"What is that supposed to mean?" she said.

"Nothing." I threw off the covers and got out of bed. Why had I said that? It's like shutting your car door while the keys are still in the ignition: you hear the door slam and feel surprised.

"Where are you going?" She raised her voice. "Don't walk away from me."

"I'm going to pee." I leaned over and scratched my ankle. "Can't I take a piss?"

"I made an appointment for us at the facility in Oshkosh. Tomorrow. Four o'clock."

"I can't go at four. I have that all day project review"

"Get someone to cover for you. Vivian. You put in enough damn hours."

I knew Vivian could, and would, fill in for me; she understood the project details as well as I did. I could duck out a little early. "OK," I said, "we can check it out." I really had to pee. "What about my father? That's not a good time to leave him alone."

"I called TJ," she said. "He's going to come over and sit with your father."

"You made all these arrangements before we agreed to it?"

"Yes." She turned off her light. "While you're up, take some more Benadryl. It'll help you sleep."

I thought about Vivian. She was going to wear her green dress and black heels. We'd discussed it.

"I'm going to take a shower," I said.

"Whatever helps," my wife said, her voice muffled by her pillow.

OUR NEIGHBOR TJ was a good friend, a real outdoors type. He'd taken my father walleye fishing, but my dad would not remember this.

"It looks like you have quite the project here," TJ said to my dad. They shook hands.

"I'm going to Canada. In the spring." My dad pointed to the maps that were spread out on the floor. "I'm going to start on the East Coast, high in the North Country, and work my way west." My dad got down on his knees and traced a finger along the maps. "I'll start here and follow the change in weather. I'll hit each lake when the ice has just thawed, and be the first to fish it." He looked at TJ, and I thought my father's long beard could use a trim. I tried to get him to shave it off, but he said he needed it—for what I was never sure. "I'll be like Adam in the Garden of Eden. Me and the Creator. The first man to see it all."

"These lures look pretty good." TJ picked one up. "You make them yourself?"

"Yes." My dad took in a sharp breath, puffed up his chest. He looked proud of his work and it made me sad.

My wife came into the room. "Dad, you and TJ are going to harvest some tomatoes and peppers, and kale from the garden, while Gary and I run an errand. You can tell him all about your trip." She turned to TJ. "Watch out for bees."

"Don't worry," I said. "I poured a gallon of ammonia in their hive. I'm sure they're all dead."

"Bees," Dad said, "you can't live with 'em, and can't live without 'em."

"You guys go," TJ said. "Take your time. Your father and I are going to have fun together."

My dad struggled to get up. TJ helped him to his feet, and my dad bent over and wiped at his knees. I remembered my dad playing softball when I was a kid. From the stands I watched him swing the bat with authority, run the bases, dust off his uniform after sliding home. His buddies greeted him with a plastic cup of beer and slaps on the back. My mom sat next me with a broad-rimmed hat to shield her face from the sun. My dad looked into the stands and blew her an exaggerated kiss. She caught it on her cheek and blew it back. She hugged my brother and me, kissed us on the top of our heads so hard that we spilled our sodas.

"Come on, let's go," my wife said giving my arm a slight tug. The black-and-white image in my head from the past was replaced with the gloomy color of the moment.

WHEN WE CAME HOME my dad and TJ were drinking beer and working on lures. They pasted hooks to pieces of painted cork, decorated with feathers my father had collected from our chicken pen. The place reeked of glue.

TJ looked up. "How'd it go?"

"I have to admit I was surprised," I said. "Much different than I thought it would be."

My dad looked at me. "Where did you go?"

"Hey," TJ said. "The bees are still there. I got stung twice, so we couldn't pick the vegetables."

"Are you all right?" my wife asked. "Do you need Benadryl or anything?"

"Naaa," TJ said. "I'm not allergic. There're just mosquito bites to me."

TJ turned down our offer to stay for dinner—he had to go home and let his dogs out. Dad talked about how much he liked TJ, how TJ helped him improve the lures, and gave him pointers on the trip. When Dad was talked out, we ate in silence. He would go through an almost manic-depressive cycle several times a day: first a lot of talk, lots of random details, and then quiet—a boat travelling through a hurricane and hitting the eye of the storm. That spot of calm worried me; one day I knew he would never make it back out.

"Who died?" my dad said.

"Not the bees," I said.

"Gas," my dad said. "I told you to use gas. You have any?"

"I have a couple of containers I use for the mowers."

"Let's do it tonight," he said. "Those tomatoes are ready to burst on the vine. We should pick them ASAP."

"So you remember the tomatoes?" I said. There were patterns to his dementia, but I was always surprised, even hopeful, when he remembered something so near-term.

"Sure, I remember."

"OK, I said, "you and me tonight. We'll gas the bees." My wife looked at me with concern. "It'll be fine," I said. "And it'll give us a chance to talk." Under the table, I gave her foot a gentle tap.

"OK," she said. "But be careful."

Betty had been very kind to my dad at first, but lately she seemed ready to pick a fight with him. I understood. We'd both thought with the kids out on their own, the dogs dead, that we'd have our freedom. The place in Oshkosh was perfect. Designed to be more of a community than a hospital. There they had art classes, concerts, a fishing pond, and even daily Mass I knew my dad, a fervent Catholic, would appreciate. But, my relief was smothered by guilt.

WE STOOD IN THE MOONLIGHT. I looked at the hole. There were no signs of the bees. I emptied the plastic gas can into the hole. "Two gallons." I said to my dad, "That should do it."

"You need to light it," he said.

"That's crazy," I said. "This should do just fine."

I don't think so." He pulled on his beard. "Remember that monk? The one who set himself on fire?"

"I've seen that picture," I said.

"He sat down in one of those yoga poses and covered himself in the gas."

"Jesus, Dad, what are you thinking about?" He never seemed unhappy, a bit lost in thought perhaps, but not discontent.

"It doesn't matter." He leaned over the bee hole. "That monk was doing just fine until he lit the gas." My dad laughed. "Then he burned like a motherfucker." He kicked at the hole. "I think this might make the bees angry, and there will be hell to pay for anyone who works around the garden. We need to burn them,"

I thought he might have a point. Two cups of ammonia was supposed to kill the hive. I poured in a gallon and it hadn't had any effect.

"You got a match?" he asked.

I pulled a lighter out of my pocket and a pack of cigarettes dropped onto the ground.

"You smoke?" he said.

"No, I don't smoke." I shrugged. "Just one or two, now and then." I put the cigarettes back in my front pocket. "Don't tell Betty," I said. "She doesn't know."

"Secrets, huh?" my dad said. "I guess we all have 'em."

He looked at his fingers. "I quit thirty years ago. Your mom made me promise. I did it cold turkey. We didn't have those patches back then. *Kents* were my brand. That small box, the castle on top, the word *Kent* in big blue letters, outlined in gold—it makes me want one right now." I was often amazed at how much he remembered. Some memories grew deep roots, while the everyday stuff dried up and blew away.

"She said she didn't want me dying too young." He rubbed his face. "Then she goes and gets cancer." He looked me in the eyes. "I wished I never quit. I miss her like all hell. We might be together now."

It had been a long time since he'd mentioned my mother as part of his past. When her name came up, he was usually wandering around the house, going from room to room, looking for her. Every time we took a drive somewhere, he'd ask if we were going to pick her up.

"Dad, stand back," I said. I leaned over and gave the disposable lighter's flint wheel a sharp spin.

The explosion was a muffled *thump*. The bright fireball knocked us both on our butts. I couldn't see my dad. After a few seconds my eyesight returned. I could smell burnt hair.

"Are you OK?" I said. His beard was singed. I ran my fingers over the top of my head and eyebrows. I too was singed.

He let out a deep breath and reached towards me. "Give me one of those cigarettes."

We sat there smoking. "They're dead now," he said.

I nodded and blew smoke in the direction of the hole.

"I can hear you and Betty fighting at night." He took a deep draw on the cigarette, held it for a few seconds, and let out the smoke. "I don't sleep well."

"It's normal, Dad. All couples fight."

"It's about me." He reached out and put a hand on my shoulder. "I understand, son." He squeezed my shoulder. His grip was stronger than I expected. "You watch yourself, though."

"What do you mean?"

"Vivian."

"How do you know about her? We work together." I wondered how the project meeting had finished up today; I made a mental note to give her a call later—it was a valid reason. "You've never met her," I said.

"No, but I'd recognize her if I ever did. You talk about her at dinners—all the time. You don't even know how much, do you?" He leaned towards me, the flame curled hair in his beard sparkled. "I see concern in Betty's face when you bring her up." He flicked away a half-spent cigarette.

I did enjoy Vivian's laugh, how it filled me with energy, made me feel young. My dad looked at me as though he could read my thoughts, and I looked away.

"Gary," my wife shouted from the deck. "Are you alright?"

"We're fine. Just talking." I could see her in the moonlight, in her night robe, arms folded, concerned. "We'll be in soon."

"You know I think about her sometimes," my dad said.

"Betty?"

"No, Vivian. What she looks like." He laughed.

"Drop it, Dad."

"I hear you and Betty fighting in your bedroom, but not much else." He stretched his back. "Your mom and I had sex right up to the end. Even after her chemo."

"Dad, come on, stop."

"You and I never had that birds and bees talk." He laughed.

"I'm a little old for that," I said.

"Can you promise me something?"

"Sure anything."

"Your brother."

"I'll take care of him," I said. "I promise."

"No," he said. "He's your older brother. He's not your problem. Don't let him tie you down. My father had a drinking problem. I think it passed to your brother." He sighed. "I'm glad he never had kids. A man can be real hard on his kids when he's been drinking." He looked up at the moon. "I want you to be free."

"Dad," I said. "I'll visit you every day."

"Every day?"

"Every day." I patted his leg. I knew I could swing down from work and spend dinnertime with him. Longer visits on the weekends. I could bring along my brother.

"It's quite a distance," he said.

"Not that far," I said.

He looked at me. "Your hair's all burnt." He touched my head. "No need to visit me. Canada is pretty far away." He asked for another cigarette and I lit one for myself—just one more. I looked up for a constellation I might recognize.

"You OK, son?"

"I'm fine. I just have a lot going on."

"Don't miss your life," he said.

I looked over at him. Sometimes his way of speaking bugged the shit out of me. "How can I possibly miss my life?" I said. "I'm in it every second." I searched my pockets for gum.

"*Be still and know that I am God.* That's from Psalm 46. I'd spend all year planning my fishing trips. I never liked ocean fishing; I was always a freshwater man. I would spend *all year* mapping out every small detail. I jumped out of bed every morning to go to work, because I couldn't wait to get on the lake and get my line in the water."

I thought we should be heading in, but wanted to stay outside.

"You know what I would do on those lakes?" he said.

"Fish?"

"I would start planning my next trip." He rubbed his hands over his face, like he was just waking up. "I've missed a lot of moments right in front of me."

It was quiet. The air was still. Something splashed in the pond, perhaps a frog. I thought about Canada: my dad and me sitting by a campfire, under the stars. A crazy idea—but maybe not.

"I miss the static," he said.

"Static?"

"Yeah, sitting on the couch, tired from an honest day's work. Drink a few beers. Watch the news, then Carson, Tom Snyder, the National Anthem—and then static. The end of the broadcast day." He shook his head. "The world would stop."

A sly grin crept across his face. "Don't tell your mom I was smoking. She thinks I quit." He struggled to his feet and I helped him up. "Aren't we supposed to be picking tomatoes?" he said.

"We can do that tomorrow." I patted him on the back. "Time for that tomorrow."

He cleared his throat. "*And even those who are yet to come, will not be remembered by those who follow.*" He stretched his arms into the sky, arched his back, and wiggled his fingers. "That's from Ecclesiastes." He sighed, and looked at me. "It all goes by too fast. Too goddamn fast."

I looked down and wondered if the bees were dead. I hoped they were.

The French Paperclip

I picked up a trombone and wondered how the darn thing worked. I moved the slide back and forth, but decided not to put my lips on the mouthpiece. This was a music store; who knew where the other mouths that blew through the instrument had been?

"Need some help?" A young man, a hipster, his hair styled in an arty fade cut. He wore narrow jeans, a white shirt, and thin black suspenders.

"I'm curious how this thing works," I said. "How do you know where the notes are?" I handed him the freakish instrument. He smiled and, without wiping the mouthpiece clean, played forty notes.

"Wow," I said, "That was Frank Zappa. *The Grand Wazoo*."

He laughed. "You and I may be the only people in this state who could identify that piece of music." He handed me the instrument and I took it, although I wasn't sure why. "You're a Zappa fan."

"A big fan," I said. "Since high school. Almost forty years now."

"Me too," he said. "I got into him my senior year of high school." He smiled. "But that was only five years ago. Have you got a favorite album?"

"That's a hard choice. *Hot Rats*, maybe. *The Grand Wazoo? Uncle Meat?*" I looked at the trombone and realized I hadn't paid attention to how the clerk made the notes. I moved the slide back and forth. "What about you?"

"I couldn't decide," he said. "I have everything he's ever recorded." He reached out and brushed something off my shoulder. "I've got every record, every CD, and every cassette tape he ever put out." The clerk put up his hands like a fisherman showing the size of a big catch. "Three-hundred-and-twenty-six recordings." The clerk folded his hands as if he were in church, about to kneel down and pray. "The cassettes are bootlegs," he said. He leaned towards me. "Probably his best work."

"I only have about fifteen of his records," I said. "A few CDs." He folded his arms, and tipped back his head. He was smug, but not condescending, assured of a victory. "I *have* seen him in concert," I said. "Four times. Once on Halloween." Zappa's Halloween concerts were famous. This kid would know that.

"Zappa died when I was a baby." He sighed. "I envy you." He looked at the instrument. "Are you thinking of buying this? It's top of the line. If you're just starting out, I'd recommend something less expensive. Or, you can rent."

"How many positions are there to make the notes?" I asked. "Are there infinite positions?"

"Just seven," he said. "The rest has to do with embouchure. You know: how tight you make your lips. It's like sex."

"How's that?" I said. I started to extend the trombone's long slide, but stopped.

"Only seven positions." He paused. "I'm just talking here about intercourse: missionary, straddle missionary, cowgirl, reverse cowgirl, doggy-style, left spoon and right spoon." He looked up and searched the ceiling. "I know it's arguable, but with the trombone, it's science. It can produce one hundred notes from just seven positions. So, it's like sex."

I handed him back the instrument.

"Here's something," he said. "The French word for paper-clip is trombone." He wiped one hand over the shiny brass and frowned. "Halloween?" he said. "How close were you? How many rows back?"

"Fifth row," I said. "Dead center."

"Damn," he said. "Well, let me know what you decide."

"I'll think about it." He nodded and walked away; I noticed he had a severe limp. He still had the instrument in his hand and was looking into the bell, as though inspecting it for some damage, or wondering where those notes came from, even though he made them. Perhaps he was imagining the fifth row.

I left the store with my question answered, but unsatisfied. I wondered now what the reverse cowgirl position was, or, for that matter, the cowgirl. I'd probably know if I saw a picture. I would never have known about the French word for paperclip.

Full Count

When I meet God, I am going to ask him two questions:
Why relativity? And why turbulence? I really believe he will
have an answer for the first.

—Werner Heisenberg

The pitch crossed the plate wide. The catcher stretched to his right and snagged it. From the mound, Hyeon-Jeong stared without emotion and waited for his teammate to throw back the ball. He saw the umpire raise his hands to signal a time-out. Rodriguez stood from his crouch behind the plate, pushed up his mask, brushed past the batter, and walked out to the mound.

"You all right, Rick?" Rodriguez asked. Hyeon-Jeong took the ball, and it felt strange in his hand, as did the sound of his name. Rick was his American name. Many Koreans working abroad shortened their names to the initials of their formal names, a way to ease complicated pronunciations Westerners could never master. Hyeon-Jeong thought of going by HJ but decided to go all the way—he picked Rick.

"I'm fine," Rick said. "Just mixing it up."

"You're one strike from winning the World Series," Rodriguez said. "Don't start messing around. We'd all like to get the hell out of here." Rick looked over his shoulder at the empty stands of the Citizen's Bank Park in Philadelphia, the Phillies home field. He was alone and knew it was his doing. He turned back to the plate; Rick neglected to give Rodriguez a signal. Rodriguez gave Rick a signal that Rick ignored, and threw another ball.

Players from both teams stood up in their dugouts, leaning over the railings, thankful for a respite from their boredom. Rick adjusted his cap and again looked at the empty seats. He thought about what the game had become, what he'd singlehandedly created since he perfected his pitch.

Rick had never encountered the knuckleball until he came to America. He first watched Steven Wright of the Red Sox, and then R.A. Dickey of the Blue Jays, throw this strange pitch. The way the ball moved, with a mind of its own, unpredictable. Rick thought it was witchcraft. His pitching coach showed him the basics. Thrown with precise control from a left-hander, at top speed, it would be unhittable. At first, Rick only occasionally took it from his toolkit to mix things up; as he got better, he used it more frequently. Rodriguez struggled to catch them. When asked about receiving these pitches, Rodriguez quoted the famed catcher, Bob Uecker, who said, "The way to catch a knuckleball is to wait until it stops rolling and then pick it up."

That was five years ago before Rick met the students.

BRAD GARDNER AND SYD JENSEN sat in their apartment, a stark basement-level, two-bedroom in West Philadelphia. They tried to keep plants, but with minimal sunlight coming through the basement window, the plants didn't survive.

The two Ph.D. candidates in physics had covered the walls with whiteboards. They filled study breaks with discussions about baseball. Equations and diagrams, meticulously detailed in multiple colors of dry-erase markers, covered the space. They described pitches in the language of mathematics. They characterized fastballs, sliders, curves, and breaking balls, by velocities, air resistance, and spin. They scribbled equations showing flight paths affected by the Magnus effect, the Karmen vortex street, fluid flow described by Bernoulli and Euler equations, scalar and vector fields, convective acceleration, and pressure gradients. They'd characterized every pitch but the knuckleball. They understood the basics, characterized the turbulent flow, but could not understand why the pitch was so hard for a pitcher to perfect, or, at least, to achieve a high consistency in its delivery.

Brad and Syd worked the stands during the Phillies' home games as food and beer vendors, attending every home game. They were also determined to visit every major league stadium in the US, and flew around the country by means of what they thought was one of the best-kept secrets on the planet: by getting part-time jobs at the airport. Working just eight hours a week in Delta's baggage claim, they got the benefit of thirty free flights. Every year.

"This guy is close," Syd said. He turned from the TV, took a swig from his bottle of Rolling Rock, and peered at his roommate's head. He reached over to touch his hair. "You getting grays, man?"

Brad pushed away Syd's hand. "Just a few. That's why I keep it so short."

"He's a hell of a reliever." Syd pointed his bottle at the TV. "Another knuckleball. I love that. He goes to that pitch a lot."

"Yeah, but more than half his knucklers are wild."

"He's throwing too fast," Syd said. "Pushing eighty miles per hour."

"I think he's leaking some rotation," Brad said. "Karmen vortex."

"He's got the seams wrong," Syd said.

"I like that he's giving it a try," Brad said. "It's gotta be hell in an open stadium with all the ambient air turbulence." Brad straightened his back. "You could quantify that," he said. "Adjust for it."

Syd laughed. "Maybe we should talk to him."

RICK JOGGED FROM THE MOUND. He watched the modest celebration in the dugout. Four games left in the season, and the Phillies last in the National League East, twenty games out, the win was inconsequential.

Rodriguez intercepted him.

"Don't give me shit." Rick said. "I struck him out."

"You're going to give me a heart attack," Rodriguez said. "I signaled a fastball."

"You caught it just fine," Rick said. He grabbed Rodriguez's shoulder. "I told you. When I get that pitch right, it's spiritual."

"If you want to find God," Rodriguez said, "Go to church." He snapped his large catcher's mitt against Rick's crotch. "Better yet, get a girlfriend."

RICK HAD AN OFF DAY and stayed home. He flipped through the *Korean Herald.* The doorbell rang. He expected to find Rodriguez with a six-pack but was met by two young men.

"Hi, Rick. My name is Brad and this is Syd." Brad held up his hands like a magician showing he had nothing up his sleeve and spoke fast. "We're physicists, and fans. We're here to help."

The word *help* triggered a memory of Rodriguez's advice when the Players Union reps came to talk to the team about a potential strike: "Never trust anyone who comes from more than fifty miles away, has a briefcase, and says that they are here to help." These guys didn't have briefcases; one of them just had a laptop under his arm, with a Phillies sticker on it.

Rick was a bit bored. He invited them in.

For an hour the guys explained their theories, describing the pitch in terms of mathematical equations. On their laptop, they flipped through graphs, gave detailed explanations of variables and constants, talked about fluid flow, and the congruence of aircraft wing surfaces with the laces on a ball. Rick's eyes glazed over. He yawned, and the guys sensed they were losing him.

Rick wanted them to leave. "This is all very interesting," he said, "but I can't imagine that you two are the first to think of these things."

"We've studied the pitch," Brad said. "There's the fundamentals…"

Syd interrupted, "Keep it well under eighty miles per hour."

"And the small elements," Brad said. "Pay attention to the breezes in the stadium. Even if it's slight, the pitch will be affected. Compensate by setting the angle slightly with the direction of the breeze. Make the laces flush. This will minimize the turbulence."

Rick looked at them. "We've researched it," Syd said. "There have been a few papers written, but they are all theoretical. No one else has taken a comprehensive approach to understanding the pitch, *with* an actual ballplayer."

"In a lab," Brad said. "A wind tunnel. What do you think?"

"I'm not saying no," Rick said. A bad habit, he thought, always being polite. "But now's not good, with the season winding down."

Brad pulled out a Sharpie. "Can I get your autograph?"

"Sure," Rick said. Brad closed his laptop and held it for Rick to sign.

"Here's our contact info." Syd handed him an index card with their phone numbers and e-mail addresses. "Call us when you want to get started."

As they settled into their car, Syd said, "I think this is a go."

Brad shook his head. "Are you kidding me? We're never going to hear from him again. I feel foolish."

"At least we tried," Syd said.

Brad held up his laptop, showing off the autograph. "Pretty cool, huh?"

Rick smiled, and thought, 'These Americans are crazy.' He took the card with their info, crumpled it into a ball, and threw it toward the wastebasket in the corner of the room. It bounced off the wall, rolling under his desk. He decided to leave it for the cleaning lady.

TWO NIGHTS LATER, Rick was called into the top of the ninth inning. His slider and curve took care of the first two batters. One more out would be another win: the end of their season. He shook off all Rodriguez's signals and smiled. He saw Rodriguez shake his head and loosen his stance behind the plate.

His first knuckler was wild, above Rodriguez's reach. Rick set for his second pitch and looked up. He noticed the stadium flags waving to the right in the slight breeze. He shut his eyes and felt the breeze on his left cheek. He tried to remember what the students had told him: angle with the breeze, or against it? He went against. The batter caught the top of the ball; it bounced down, hit the plate, and went straight into Rodriguez's glove.

The umpire inspected the ball and gave Rodriguez a fresh one to toss back to Rick.

Rick caught it and thought, *with the breeze.* His next pitch danced side to side and the batter swung over it. The next pitch followed the same trajectory. The batter swung, thinking to hit the slow pitch out of the park, but caught only air. The batter looked at Rodriguez. "What the hell was that?" Rodriguez shrugged.

When he came in from the mound, Rodriguez gave Rick a high five. "I think I felt him man," Rodriguez said.

"Who?" Rick asked.

"That last pitch," Rodriguez said. "I felt God."

"It's something, huh?" Rick went home that night, crawled under his desk, and retrieved the crumpled index card.

BRAD AND SYD SET UP equipment in the university's wind tunnel: anemometers to measure micro-changes in ambient wind speed, infrared thermometers to record temperature gradients, manometers for atmospheric pressures, hygrometers for the moisture content in the air, and high-speed video equipment. Rick threw pitches for them: hundreds of different release angles, and numerous pitch grips, varied speeds, all calibrated with the conditions found in a stadium. In the wind tunnel, they could control the conditions and adjust micro-parameters.

Each round of test throws was preceded by a conference with the two students, who'd tell Rick the exact conditions he needed to compensate for. They logged data, checked and adjusted Rick's technique, and went again. Rick was excited by the progress; he could feel a flow with the pitch. Tired of delays from picking up balls that bounced off the target, Rick suggested that Rodriguez come in to catch.

The *Philadelphia Inquirer* ran a short piece on the experiment in the sports section, and a day later, the viewing room outside the lab was filled with technicians who ran the equipment, other students who wanted to watch the action, Brad and Syd's professors, and Jim Daniels, the cantankerous Phillies owner, who was worried that all the extra pitching might wreck Rick's arm. Daniels flew Ben Simmons, the team's pitching coach, up from his vacation home in Florida to monitor the experiment.

"Rick," Daniels said after watching two hours of pitching. "I think this needs to stop."

"I'm OK. I'm only clocking fifty or sixty miles per hour." Rick swung his arm in a circle. "I could do this all day."

Simmons nodded, "He'll be fine. No harm." He grabbed his jacket. "I'm going back to the beach."

After seven more days, Rick got to the point where he didn't need the equipment and numbers to fine-tune the pitch; he could feel it all in his gut. He could determine the exact throwing force and trajectory of the release angle, and he knew when, and where, it would zig, zag, and dip.

Syd looked at Brad and said, "I wonder what he's thinking when he throws?"

Gary Bender, a neuroscience student, pushed between Brad and Syd. "You know we can find that out."

Rick was back in the wind tunnel two days later and scratched his head. "Hey," Brad said into the control room's microphone. "No scratching. You'll screw up the sensors." Rick refused to shave his head, as they had asked, but was fine with a short buzz cut. Thirty small, silver, metallic transmitters, each the size of a dime, were fastened to his head.

Jim Daniels came into the room and looked at Rick. "So, what the hell is this?" Daniels said. Now, with two of his players involved, he was keeping an eye on the experiment. He threatened to pull Rick and Rodriguez from the project unless the University banned spectators, other than essential scientists and technicians. He emphasized that there be no reporters. He didn't want his team to become some sort of joke in the press, or an off-season freak show.

Gary Bender explained. "They're small sensors I've developed, that pick up neural-net patterns in Rick's brain. They transmit the data to our computer, right here." Gary tapped his laptop.

"So, you're messing with his brain?" Daniels said. "You going to electrocute my pitcher?"

"No chance of that," Gary said. "Think of it like an MRI. Each of the thirty connectors is monitoring Rick's sensory cortex. We can pick up neural activity from all his body parts, even his lips, cheeks, nose…every body part. It's perfectly safe."

Daniels poked a finger into Gary's chest, "It better be."

Over three days they calibrated Rick, told him what environmental changes were made, showed him his brain patterns, and tuned his motions to what his body was perceiving. As the changes to air movement and temperature were adjusted down to subtle fluctuations, Rick initially had difficulty registering them. Syd recommended that he lick his lips and wet his cheeks and forehead with spit to heighten his sensitivity. The promptness of the technique's effect surprised the young scientists.

"We may be done here," Brad said.

Rick stood on the makeshift mound and licked his lips. He recalled his tongue brushing across Seung-ah's mouth, the way her upper lip stood out at a severe angle when she was serious, but how her smile stretched it across her face, the edges pointing to her dimples—a glorious magic trick that he knew was forever lost.

The next ten pitches were all wild, out of Rodriguez's reach.

Syd and Gary entered the wind tunnel. "Rick, what's wrong?" Syd said.

"What are you thinking about?" Gary said.

Rick looked at his feet. "I'm a little embarrassed."

Rodriguez put his arm on Rick's shoulder. "You alright, man? Getting tired of this shit?"

"I was thinking about my old girlfriend…" Rick stopped.

"She died," Rodriguez said. He patted Rick on the back.

"I'm sorry to hear that," said Brad.

"You're distracting yourself," Gary said. "Your prefrontal cortex is overloading your sensory cortex." Gary squinted. "You ever meditate?"

"In South Korea, I was raised a Buddhist."

"Just settle down," Gary said. "Stay in the moment, take a few slow inhales, and follow your breath."

"I don't need a meditation lesson from you," Rick said.

"Right," Gary said. "Of course not."

In the wind tunnel, Rick imagined that he was back at the Bongeunsa Temple in Seoul. His rear resting on his heels, an erect back, with each exhale he emptied his mind.

"Holy shit," Gary said from the viewing booth. "His prefrontal cortex has flatlined. Totally flatlined." Gary pointed at the laptop screen. "He's stopped his thought."

"This is amazing. Why haven't I thought of this before?"

In the lab, Rick opened his eyes and threw a pitch. It was perfect. The young scientists changed every environmental parameter, and Rick threw perfect pitches, speed, angle, lace orientation, and release point, all perfectly adjusted. Two hundred perfect knuckleballs.

"He's better than a machine," Brad said.

"He *is* a machine," Syd said.

Over the next week, Rick and Rodriguez worked out a new set of pitching signs. They developed nine different and nuanced knuckleballs. The system was the reverse of traditional baseball norms: Rick gave the sign to Rodriguez.

"Are we going to publish?" Brad said. He extended a high five.

"You bet," Syd said. He slapped back with enthusiasm.

Brad slumped. "Did we sign a non-disclosure agreement?"

Syd shrugged. "We signed a lot of papers."

ON APRIL 2nd, Rick started for the Phillies in the season opener. He pitched a no-hitter. Rick was never hit again.

After his first game, Rick was put on the rotation for starting pitchers, seeing the field every three to five games. Each time he pitched; the opposing team failed to get a single player on base. Two months into the season Rick passed Nolan Ryan's lifetime record of seven perfect games.

Rick pitched back-to-back games in the postseason, winning the Phillies the National League Pennant. He played every game at the end of the postseason, credited with leading the Phils to their first World Series victory in fifteen years. After his last pitch, his teammates rushed from the dugout and carried Rick off the field on their shoulders.

Rick started the next season's opener with a no-hitter. The team's pitching coach, Ben Simmons was put in a tough spot. The other pitchers started to grumble, wanting to be traded if they didn't play. He decided to put an end to Rick's streak, and arranged to have him start every game until his arm gave out. Jim Daniels voiced no objections to this, all business metrics were up: attendance, concession sales, viewers, advertising, and merchandising. The entire league was flush with cash; Rick's rising tide raised all the league's boats. His bubble grew. When Rick pitched, games sold out. Even the Milwaukee Brewers, a team in a constant state of rebuilding, with the lowest attendance in the league, sold out Miller Park when Rick pitched.

Fifteen games into the season Rick stood on the field with Rodriguez. Rick waved his hat at the cheering fans.

"They love me," Rick said.

Rodriguez shook his head. "They're not here to see you win. They want to watch you get hit."

Rick continued to wave his hat. "Don't hold your breath folks. Not gonna happen."

"The guys are hoping for the same thing," Rodriguez said. "Maybe you should let one game go."

"Look at my feet," Rick said. "I'm not barefoot. No way." Rodriguez nodded and turned to walk away. "Hey," Rick shouted. "You better not drop any pitches."

Rick pitched every game of the season and took the Phils to their first consecutive World Series wins.

At the final Series game in the next season, Rick took the mound in the ninth to boos, shouts: *Get off the field. Go back to Korea. Booo!* Rick ignored the crowd's admonishments and delivered the Phillies their third consecutive Series win.

The next season, the decline in attendance was abrupt. People stopped showing up. Every team tried, but Rick's performance could not be replicated by any of the other league's pitching staff. No one cared about any of their team's games and the season's outcome was a foregone conclusion. The world's interest in seeing Rick get hit vanished.

Brad and Syd no longer occupied their seats in the owner's box. Locked out from publishing their findings for ten more years, they burned all their notes, deleted all data, erased files, wiped all hard drives clean. One drunken night, they smashed a pile of thumb drives with an aluminum bat. They'd stopped watching the sport altogether.

By November, there was a frenzied hype before the final game of the Series. Al James, the Cubs' center fielder, the league homerun leader, vowed to get a hit. A man of faith, he told the press he prayed to Jesus, and that the Lord spoke to him, and assured him he would beat this foreigner—this demon, who must have made a deal with the Devil. He asked the world to pray with him.

THE PHILLIES WERE AHEAD by three runs when Rick trotted from the dugout to the mound in the top of the ninth. He was greeted with boos and shouts. Rick waved off Rodriguez's warm up throws. After the first two outs, James walked from the batter's box. He swung three bats. The stadium erupted in cheers. He discarded two of the bats and knelt. He held his bat overhead, looked skyward, and prayed. The fans went silent. He stood and walked to the plate. The fans cursed Rick and cheered James. Rick motioned for a time out.

Rick turned away from home plate and raised his hands in the air. He mimicked James's motions. He turned with his outstretched arms to each section of the stands. The intensity of the fans' displeasure grew. A unified chant erupted: *Diablo. Diablo. Diablo.* Rick turned to the players on the field and waved both his arms downward. He did the motion again, and again. He yelled at his team, "Sit down, sit down." The other players on the field looked at each other, then one by one, they sat at their positions.

Three pitches later, James went down swinging, and the Phillies won their fourth Series. Rick threw his hat in the air, stretching out his open arms towards his teammates. No one joined him on the field. Rick walked to the players as they came off the field, his arm, extended for a shake, was brushed aside. Rick looked at Rodriguez. The catcher took a few steps towards Rick, then turned, and left the field. The stadium emptied in silence. Rick retrieved his hat, walked to the mound, and stood on the field for an hour, alone.

BEFORE THE START OF THE NEXT SEASON, the baseball commissioner called a mandatory meeting with the owners. Jim Daniels guessed what the commissioner wanted to discuss, and he was ready to make concessions. Daniels knew that before long the financial drought that the other teams experienced would affect the Phillies.

The commissioner started the meeting with a prepared statement, signed by all the other owners. They *demanded* that Daniels drop Rick back to a normal pitching rotation.

"Demand?" Daniels said. "Demand?" He leaned in. "No one here is in any position to *demand* me to do anything. I'm not violating any bylaws. I might have considered this if you asked but screw you all. I'll do as I please." Daniels stood up. "Excuse me gentlemen, I'm done here."

News of the meeting was leaked to the press.

Daniels hired a roomful of lawyers in the offseason. Players sued to get out of their contracts, the league filed litigation against him, and the City of Philadelphia threatened to end the twenty-year tax holiday on the stadium's property lease.

Rick took the field alone at the start of the next season. Other than Rodriguez, Daniels had ordered that no other players take the field. After the fifth game, Daniels had Rick replaced at-bat with a permanent pinch-hitter. His prize player had become nothing more than a target to the other pitchers.

The Phillies won every game and were one strike away from winning their fifth series.

Rick stood on the home field mound, lost in thought. The stadium was quiet. A sparsely attended game. The umpire yelled at him. *Play Ball!*

Rick nodded, failed to give Rodríguez a signal, and threw a wild pitch that his catcher struggled to contain. The umpire shouted, "Ball." It was the first time Rick threw anything except a strike for five years.

Three pitches later the batter walked. Rick watched his coach bark orders, and the rest of his team spring from the dugout and take their positions. It was the first time this year his team needed to take the field.

Eight pitches later the bases were loaded. This event was breaking news on every television station; the bars and home TVs all tuned into the game. It was a new record, fifty-two million viewers, within minutes. Marketers sprang into action to sell time. Public service announcements, which had become the bane of baseball games, were pushed to the side, replaced by thirty-second commercials that went for top dollar.

Viewers watched the conference at the mound. Rick stood still, as George Henry, the Phillies' manager, and Rodriguez, consulted with Rick. Henry threatened to pull him, but Rick knew that would never happen, baseball was a business; and for the first time in a long time, in this moment, business was good, and he was the star product.

The world watched. Fans trickled into the stadium. With the bases loaded, two outs in the bottom of the ninth, a full count, and the Phillies leading the fourth game, poised for a win that would make them the first team to take the World Series five years in a row since the Yankees in the early fifties.

Rick settled on the mound.

It started to rain. It rained hard.

"*NAE-GA NEO-REUL A-REO?*" Rick looked at the man. The stranger sat down on a barstool next to him.

"Do you know me?" Rick said in Korean.

"Yes," the man said, also in Korean, "I do know who you are." The bar was in the sticks of South Jersey, where Rick thought he could be alone, to think. "You're Hyeon-Jeong Kim."

Rick guessed from the man's accent he was from a southern province: one of the slow islands of Korea.

"I've followed your career since your days with the Twins in Seoul," the man said. "You are a hero back home. Let me buy you a beer. Might we continue speaking in Korean, I need the practice."

Rick nodded.

"Aren't you violating curfew or something?" the man said. "Tomorrow's the final game."

"It's just game four," Rick said. "Still three more games left."

"Right," the man said. The bartender set two drafts in front of them and scraped a ten off the bar.

"Let's toast," the man said, raising his mug. "To perfection." Rick took a sip of his drink. "I'm not one for small talk," the man said, "I have to ask. Why do you look so down?"

"I'm…just feeling strange." Rick looked into his beer. "Like a ghost in my own life."

The man took a drink. "I met Ansel Adams once," he said. "In the early eighties, right before he died. It was at a retrospective of his work in New York."

Rick raised his mug to his lips. "I have no idea who that is."

"You do, but it doesn't matter," the man said. "He was a great photographer. I walk over and tell him I'm from Korea. A big fan."

The bartender left the change and Rick slid him a two-dollar tip.

"Nice thing to say," Rick said, detached.

"I tell Adams, Ansel Adams, the greatest photographer of our time, his pictures are vivid. Puts me right there. You know what he says to me?"

"No."

"He tells me someday he'd like to see them himself. Strange, right? So I say, what are you talking about? You have been all these places. You took all these pictures."

"I might want to be alone here," Rick said.

"You don't," the man said. "I'm here. The universe has put me right here so that I can tell you what he told me."

Rick watched the man take a quick swig. Beer dripped down his chin.

"Ansel Adams tells me he never had a chance to see any of these places. He says that it was all about framing, and composition, and F-stops, and light filters, and when he looks at these pictures, it were as though he was never there to see these places. He said he'd like to go back and see them, without a camera. You know what he tells me next?"

Rick set down his empty mug on the bar. "What?"

"He says when he thinks about being at those places, it was as if he'd been a ghost. Not really there at all."

Rick motioned for the bartender to bring two more. "I think I have heard of him."

"Of course you know him, but that's not important," the man said. "His photographs were a thing of perfection. But they are a representation of reality. Not reality. Creating these illusions, Adams doesn't feel real himself. He's disconnected, disembodied, missing it—a ghost in his own life."

"Philosopher, huh?

"I dabble here and there," he said. "You are a thing of perfection: six feet tall, two hundred pounds of muscle, a solitary man. A machine on the mound and look what it's done to the game."

"Destroyed the thing I love." Rick heard himself say the word in Korean—*salang*: love. The sport, his fame, took his girl back home. Seung-ah. Not his girl anymore, there had been no time for her back then. He remembered their last tearful phone call. He thought he was setting her free, setting them both free. Her final release came on the Mapo Bridge over the Han River; *The Bridge of Life*, where she ended her pain, her shattered body fished from the river weeks later. Rick placed his hand on his chest, a gesture he performed countless times during the National Anthem. Now, he wanted to dig his fingers in, rip out his heart, and throw it against the wall at one hundred miles per hour, so he could join the dead.

"Hey." The man poked him in the shoulder. "Yes. Not on purpose. Not your fault. You did what anyone else would do. I saw you play in Seoul many times. I was sad but proud, you got the chance to come to the U.S., to pitch in the big leagues."

Rick noticed the man's face. "Was one of your parents American?"

"They both were," the man said. "I was born in Wisconsin. My father worked in a paper mill. My mother was a teacher. I have no Korean blood. You see."

"Mind reader?" Rick said.

"I look Asian. But my hair is straightened and, well, I'm over fifty, it's dyed black. My eyes were surgically modified. My language…now I even think in Korean. I can only speak broken English." The man tried to get the bartender's attention. "As a young man, I had my reasons for leaving America, for changing how I look."

"So now you're out of hiding?" Rick said.

"Just hidden in plain sight," the man said. "I have my reasons."

The bartender looked at their beers and leaned in. "What can I get you?"

Rick heard the man say, "Fries."

The bartender looked at Rick. "What do you want?"

"Fries," Rick said. "A basket of fries."

"You got it, champ."

"So, you came to America," the man said, "and were a pretty good relief pitcher. Then you threw that perfect knuckler and never got hit again. The Phils started you, and your first game was a no-hitter. Bradley got sick and they started you again—the very next night. You threw another no hitter and got the Phils into the playoffs. You pitched every game in the series, all no hitters and won your first championship. Two years later, they put you in every game and the league comes down on the Phils, demanding they use other pitchers."

"Yes, that caused quite a commotion."

"All your team ever needed to do," the man said, "was get one run. So, you won your second series."

"Yes," Rick said. "Good for the team but bad for baseball."

"Exciting at first. Then the game got boring. No fans. No advertisers. Now you are about to take a fifth. What do you have now, three-hundred-and-sixty wins? I remember the celebration when you passed Carlton. The news when you slipped by Clemens and Maddox."

He grabbed Rick's arm. "Then you passed Cy Young. I know you must be thinking about that." Rick felt the man's fingers dig into his arm, and Rick pulled away. "It took Young twenty-two years to win five-hundred-and-eleven games. You did it in just four."

"Why are you here?" Rick said.

"Some unfinished business," the man said. "What is your earliest childhood memory?"

Rick looked across the bar at his own reflection in the mirror. "My father."

"The shipbuilder."

"How do you know my father was a shipbuilder?"

"Like I said, I followed you in Seoul. I read all about you." The man smiled. "But your father was a degreed architect. A strange career path, don't you think?"

"I sat by my father the day he died," Rick said. "Just last year. I asked him why he studied architecture, and he told me it was because he was born just after the war. His city had been destroyed during the occupation. He spent most of his youth rebuilding it, and he wanted to study architecture to go back and continue." Rick paused. "To make it something better."

"But he never got back."

"He got hired by Hyundai to build ships. Then he became a project manager to build oil rigs."

The bartender delivered the fries and told Rick to be careful because the plate was hot. Rick asked for two more beers.

"A funny thing though," Rick said. He seemed happy. Not filled with regret. He was determined to beat the cancer and finally go back to his town. To build."

"Yes," the man said. "There was still work to be done. He had a goal. A purpose. A future."

"But he died."

"What is your earliest childhood memory? With your father?"

Rick looked at his reflection in the mirror. "I remember sitting on my father's lap, I may have only been around seven years old and my father showed me pictures of his town. Black and white photos, crumbled buildings, people digging, women hugging children. He swore to go back someday. I wanted to go back there with him."

"But baseball entered your life."

"Yes. And he died."

"And at university, you studied…?"

"Also architecture," Rick said.

"There have been maybe twenty Korean ball players here in the States," the man said. "Chen Ho Park was the first, a pitcher like you, built like you, the greatest. Up to now. Have you seen the Koi fish mural in Ihwa?"

"I have," Rick said. "I actually walked through the area with my father a few months before he died. He loved going there."

"Good. The Koi was one of the most famous murals in the world, amazing 3D effect. But it's not there anymore."

"I've heard about that in the news."

"That part of Seoul was a dreary place, an economically depressed community," the man said. "So, a group of artists started painting the murals and the area became famous. Many tourists traveled to see them—thousands every year. Lots of small shops popped up. The murals seemed to do their job. But the locals hated it: all the people taking pictures, being loud. So, one night they poured paint over the mural and destroyed it. In protest. They didn't want gentrification; they wanted their quiet community."

"How do you know this?"

The man leaned over and whispered. "Between you and me, I know the man who dumped the paint."

"Did it work?"

"Time will tell. There is chatter they are going to repaint the mural." The man stood up. "I have to go."

"But let's continue to talk," Rick said.

"No," the man said. "It's getting late for me. But not too late for you." Rick felt the man's hand on his shoulder, a gentle touch. "Do you remember the name of your father's town?"

Rick tried to recall it, but the name was hidden in a blind spot. "I don't," he said.

"That's too bad." The man paused. "Remember your name, your real name, what it means. Hyeon-Jeong: virtuous, worthy, able, shining, loyal." He bowed to Rick, turned, and headed to the door.

Rick sat, finished his drinks and most of the fries. He stood up and threw a twenty on the bar.

The bartender rushed over. "Hey, champ. Are you OK to drive? You've had quite a few."

"I'll be fine." Rick pointed to the door. "The other guy did his share of the drinking."

The bartender looked over Rick's shoulder, then back at Rick "You OK, champ? Let me call you a cab."

"I'm good," Rick said.

"Congrats, man, on number five." The bartender gave Rick two thumbs-up.

Rick nodded and whispered, "Fat lady hasn't sung yet." In his mind he translated the phrase into Korean; what came of it made him laugh.

THE STADIUM FILLED UP, people rushed in to see, to be there. The rain delay was over. The crew finished rolling back the tarp. Rick stood on the mound and noticed the noise, the cheers, the dirt under his feet, as he scraped the ground with his left foot, the laces of the ball as he rolled it in his glove. His teammates yelled encouraging words from the field and dugout. The bases were loaded.

He looked at the wetness of the stadium. Water drops sparkled in the bright lights. He remembered sitting in the park next to the Han River at sunset with Seung-ah, as the sun dripped a thousand dancing fireflies on the river's surface.

Images fused in his mind: the man in the bar, Seung-ah's descent, his father's last breath. He heard the umpire yell, "Play ball!" The signal came from Rodriguez, four fingers down: his fastest knuckler. Rick nodded and ignored it.

When it left his fingertips, Rick knew three things: the fastball would clock at 90 miles per hour and cross the plate at the batter's sweet spot, the name of his father's hometown was Gimje, and it was the last pitch he would ever throw.

The Blue Blazer

Adam Lipari sat alone in the conference room. He brushed a short white hair off the sleeve of the blue blazer his grandmother had given him for the interview. The hair was from his dog, Bartholomew, a gentle, eleven-year-old pit bull. "You can't go wrong with a blue blazer," his grandmother said. She'd bought it on sale at Goodwill, in decent condition, and his size: 42 regular, for $9.99.

The digital clock on the wall read 10:38. The interview was supposed to start at 10:30. This made Adam nervous, he wondered if he'd already lost the job. He smoothed down the jacket and felt something in the breast pocket. With two fingers he took out the contents: a piece of paper wrapped around a one-hundred-dollar bill. In small, precise printing the unfolded note said: *Pop-Pop, you always had a few bucks for me; this is for you, in case you need it.*

Adam looked at the money and thought of meth. Two months out of his third stint in rehab, he felt that familiar sensation—a low-flying panic attack. He prayed for strength. The conference room door opened. Adam returned the money and note into his pocket. He stood to shake hands. He wondered about the money.

AT EIGHTY-TWO, AFTER A perfect drive from the ninth tee, Barry Robinson collapsed. While his ball made a 6.3-second flight to the green, his undiagnosed aortic aneurysm ruptured, and he bled to death.

Ahead of the funeral service Barry's immediate family: his wife, two sons, their spouses, and five grandsons, were given time for a private viewing. They each had a few moments alone in front of the open casket to speak final words to the body.

Barry's wife had dressed him in his favorite blue blazer. Years ago, she begged him to get rid of it. He said, "No. I'll never get rid of this blazer; I want to be buried in it." And he was.

His middle grandson, the quiet one, knelt by the casket and whispered in Barry's lifeless ear. He slipped something into his grandfather's top breast pocket.

After hundreds of *I'm sorry for your losses*, a church service, profound and mundane speakers, a tearjerker slide show, a pretty good buffet, and a short ride in a hearse, Barry's casket was wheeled into the crematorium.

The funeral director, a Robin Hood of sorts, had been bending the rules for decades. He removed all the jewelry and clothing from bodies before the burn. He enjoyed imagining someone buying one-carat diamond earrings for $8.99, or a platinum watch for $6.85.

Barry's corpse had embalming fluid seepage from a hole in the left leg made during the autopsy. The pants were damaged but the blazer was in good shape. The funeral director removed and folded it. He placed it in the box for his weekly thrift store run. He rotated deliveries to avoid notice—that week was Goodwill.

AT 12:15, ADAM'S GRANDMOTHER sat in the coffee shop, the designated meet-up spot, and waited for her grandson to walk through the door. Her heart was broken so many times: a philandering husband, a dead daughter, and the last of her legacy, Adam, was struggling. She worried that he might not show; a bad interview and he might be out using. He was supposed to be there at noon. She alternated glances between the café clock and her Bible.

When Adam walked past the glass window of the café she stood and thought through a litany of prepared responses: *There will be other opportunities. Don't worry it just means God has something better planned. At least you got some good interviewing practice.*

He burst through the door, greeted her with a broad smile and handed her a bouquet of fresh flowers. She didn't have to ask how it went and gave him a big hug. He told her the manager said of all the candidates, he was the best qualified, and the best dressed, and he starts on Monday. Adam told his grandmother he was taking her around the corner to her favorite Italian restaurant for a proper lunch. "Where did you get the money?" she asked with concern.

As they strode down the sunny street Adam told her about the blazer's pocket. "Kind of like magic," he said.

"That's not magic," she said. "That's God."

At the restaurant's entrance, Adam held the door for his grandmother. They paused as a warm surge of aromas: home-made marinara sauce, roasted garlic, and fresh baked bread, washed away their burdens.

The *maître d'* asked Adam if he wanted him to hang up his jacket. "No," Adam said. "I'll keep it on."

Frames

His decision to retire surprised, even shocked, many of his coworkers, but was met with approval from his boss. At fifty-seven, Patrick Isaacs was at an awkward age. He loved what he did as a Research and Engineering Manager, and he continued to drive good business results, but when he applied for other jobs, he was told his runway was too short. He began to think of himself as that Tupperware container of food in the back of the refrigerator: not good enough to eat, not bad enough to throw out.

He'd assumed he would work until he was found at his desk, as did his father and grandfather, dead of a heart attack. Predestined to leave the world with this badge of honor. Instead, he ate retirement cake, shook a lot of hands, listened to speeches about his legacy, gave his own reflections on his career, had drinks with the boys, and then, before walking out after thirty-five years, turned in his computer, company phone, corporate credit card, and company ID. His heart was beating just fine.

Patrick and his wife, Helen, entered the crowded restaurant with their friends, Larry and Beth, for their regular first Friday dinner outing. Though neighbors, except for this planned get-together, they rarely saw each other. This Friday night happened to coincide with Patrick's retirement.

The restaurant was new; at least it had a new name: The Brindled Bovinae. The previous owners, a couple, had run the old place, Jenny's Paper City Table, into the ground. Bankrupt. They were now divorced. The new owners, two brothers from Chicago, transformed the place from a humdrum Wisconsin supper club into a big city steakhouse. After an initial buzz of excitement, in seven months they would also be out of business. A price point that strained against the community's tight purse strings, slow service, the elk meat scare—even the restaurant's name confused the community. Local residents would never agree on the pronunciation, or what it meant.

Patrick held open the entrance door. He had been there many times but felt a difference. The new door had a significant weight. He stood and let an elderly couple go in ahead of him. He followed into the vestibule. The elderly man returned the polite gesture, and he held the next door for him.

Patrick was taken aback by the interior. The worn-out, non-descript interior, simple tables, the comforting '50s décor, all of it was gone. Large, exposed beams ran along the high ceiling. Immense, ancient wrought iron chandeliers lit the room with electrical fixtures that mimicked candles; a large bar with an ornate mirror that reached the ceiling commanded the length of the room. Patrick had the impression of a gothic castle, or perhaps a turn-of-the-century pub. A name came to Patrick. The Spouter Inn. A stray detail. He remembered it from Moby Dick, recalling a high school assignment to read the book. He never finished it but knew the book was somewhere in the house. He decided to pick it back up and add it to his list. Now that he had the time to read it, to do it justice.

Patrick scanned the crowd and saw Helen motioning to him from the far end. He squeezed through the crowd in her direction. A man standing at the bar made brief eye contact, and Patrick conferred a casual nod. The man returned the gesture and anticipated a response from Patrick. He passed, without any exchange, and saw the man's expression drop to disappointment and then a scowl. Patrick thought he might have bumped into him, but there had been no physical contact.

Patrick looked over the menu, noting the prices, as was his habit. The place was expensive—change had its cost—but he knew he would not be paying; after the check arrived, he would take out his wallet and be told to put it away. Larry would grab the tab as a friendly gesture to congratulate him on his retirement. The waiter came to take their drink order. Helen suggested mojitos, but Larry insisted on starting with champagne—not just a glass, a whole bottle.

"So, this is a surprise," Larry said. "Very unexpected. What are your plans?"

"Well…" Patrick felt he had answered the question a hundred times leading up to this moment. "I'm looking to spend more time with the grandkids. Some gardening. A lot of bike riding. Paint the two porches on the house. Reading. Maybe some travel."

"We're going to spend a month in Italy," Helen said. She had four years of teaching high school English ahead of her until her pension was fully vested.

"Well," Patrick said, "we're thinking about that. We have to consider living on a limited income."

Larry waved a dismissive hand in the air. "Don't worry about the budget tonight. Dinner is on us." Patrick's drink emptied a little too quickly. He inspected his glass. It had a large bowl but was shallow. A way for the owners to skimp on the drinks, save money. He was relieved that Larry ordered a bottle. He now felt like drinking.

The waitress repeated their orders, "Four prime ribs, two rare, and one medium." She looked at Patrick. "Are you sure well done?"

"Yes, I'm sure," Patrick said.

Patrick felt a large hand grab and shake his shoulder. He turned to see the man from the bar. He was holding a drink;

Patrick guessed it was a scotch and not his first. "Jimmy," the man said, "it's me, Ben. Why'd you walk past me like that?"

"I'm sorry," Patrick said, "I think you have me mixed up with someone else."

"No way. You're Jimmy Franklin. Christ, Jimmy, you served under me in the Reserves. For what, four years?"

"Sorry, man, that's not me. My name is Patrick Isaacs, and I've never been in the service, at all."

The man looked at him, and the others at the table. "You OK, Jimmy?"

"You have me mixed up with someone else."

The man looked hurt. "You're not Jimmy Franklin?"

"I'm not."

"Shit man, you must have a twin in the world." The man took a long drink of his scotch. "Sorry to interrupt your dinner, folks." He turned to go, then turned back. "Next round on me. Still drinking those old Rob Roys, Jimmy?"

Patrick said, "That's not necessary, but thanks."

"I insist." He left. Patrick watched the man navigate through the crowd and noticed he struggled with a stiff limp. He concluded one of his legs was a prosthetic—an injury from abroad? Everyone at the table looked at Patrick. None of them knew what was in a Rob Roy, but they knew it was Patrick's drink of choice.

Patrick tipped his glass and finished the last drops of his champagne. "Strange huh?"

"Really strange," Beth said. "Don't all look at once, but he's obviously talking about you to his friends. He doesn't look happy." Larry reached with the bottle to refill Patrick's glass. "Patrick, do you have anything you want to tell us?"

Helen leaned in. "This happens all the time to him."

"This is the third time," Patrick said. He told his friends about the others. At a Cuban restaurant in South Beach, a guy swore Patrick was Javier Alezzi, a Florida real estate mogul. A woman in northern California approached Patrick and Helen as they stared off a roadside vista asserting he was Scott Barber, the plumber who renovated their bathroom.

"I guess I have that kind of face," Patrick said.

Dinner arrived and Isaacs looked at his meat, wet with blood, the same as all the others. He kept his displeasure and disgust to himself.

PATRICK WOKE ON HIS FIRST DAY of retirement; he showered, skipped shaving for the third day, and examined his face in the mirror. He frowned at the gray already showing in his new beard, and rubbed his chin, sliding his thumb over the visible scar from a childhood fall. He still remembered the pain when the doctor put in the six stitches. Dressed in his normal business casual attire, he joined Helen in the kitchen. Steam drifted from the mug of coffee that she had prepared for him.

She looked at him. "My, my, aren't we all spiffed up," She'd expected that he'd be dressed in his typical Saturday jeans and a Green Bay Packers t-shirt.

"It's a workday for everybody else in the world," he said.

"You may be in the wrong kind of work clothes," she said, pointing to several yellow Post-it notes on the kitchen counter. "I left a few things for you to do. I think it's a good time for us to de-clutter the place. Starting with those boxes in the back of the basement."

"What boxes?" He knew their basement was filled with boxes; he didn't know which ones she meant.

"The ones in the way back," she said. "The way-way back."

"What's in them?"

"That's my point," she said. "We put them back there when we moved into this place sixteen years ago. I doubt it's anything we need or want."

After she'd left for work, he looked at the notes: "Water the plants. Buy porch paint. I'll be home by five. Make grilled cheese for dinner. One yellow post-it with the word: BOXES!"

Patrick sat on the back deck and stared at the sky and his property. He loved the six-acre farmette, or, as his father might have called it, a gentleman's farm: big trees, several outbuildings, and a huge red barn. Could be a lifetime of projects or could just be a place to sit and enjoy. Birds were busy at the deck's many feeders. They ignored his presence.

He finished his third cup of coffee and tried to clear a head fog. He already missed the stress-induced adrenaline rush from back-to-back meetings, endless e-mails, weekly budget cuts, and the drama of the day's fire. He thought more coffee would help.

He made a second pot, half a typical day's intake. At the office, he drank it all day long, never without a mug in his hand. He thought he should cut back, for his heart, but not today.

The July sun was bright, and he wondered if it would be humid. What should he do? Bike riding? Gardening? Paint the porches? None of the above? The thing he wanted to do was stay in place. He remembered from high school physics: Work = Force x Distance. He hypothesized: No Work = No Force x No Distance. The science made sense. What was wrong with that plan?

He enjoyed stillness. Sit, read, watch birds from the deck, listen to music. Why did Helen have this deep desire to live abroad? Wouldn't it be the same? Sitting on another deck somewhere, seeing a different view; after a while, it would become the same thing. The view at home would be so much cheaper.

That damn question: What are you going to do? What are you going to do? What are you going to do? His honest answer was socially unacceptable. Nothing. Nothing. Nothing. The one he gave worked: the grandkids, home projects, travel. The thought of it started the tape even though no one was there to hear. Perhaps he would add volunteering to the list.

The HR counselor at work, a thoughtful man, a Buddhist, told him to expect a transition period. Perhaps a month or two, where he might go through the denial-anger-depression cycle before discovering who he was, independent of his career. He had given Patrick a folder of helpful articles on the topic, some reading to begin this new phase of life.

Patrick sipped his coffee and opened the folder. He scanned the articles. Key points from St. John of the Cross's Dark Night of the Soul, an excerpt of Ram Dass's Be Here Now, a summary of William Bridges' Managing Transitions, an exegesis of Ecclesiastes. A list of about twenty other book recommendations. He swirled in the ideas. For centuries, philosophers and theologians have been trying to answer the question of finding personal identity in the midst of change. Why are we here? You are not what you own. You are not what you do. You are not your physical appearance. You are not your emotions. You are not your thoughts. Your true self is in the space between your thoughts, which is where you connect to the collective consciousness and the stardust from which we all came, and where we shall all return. It felt unreal, disconnected, and pointless. Patrick's heart sped up. He felt adrift. He already missed the anchor of work. He resolved to find the space between thoughts.

He settled in, motionless on the deck, but sweat started on his forehead and arms. The unfinished basement below their one-hundred-year-old farmhouse would be twenty degrees cooler, and he decided to check out the boxes—just to look at them. He walked through the garage to the basement's separate entrance. He went down the steps.

The first room was the largest. A makeshift setup: a sitting area, an old bed, some shelves, a desk, and thrift store lamps. They'd never used it unless their house was overflowing with family visitors from back East, which had not happened for years. He noted that the walls looked good. He ran a finger over the concrete. Cool as he anticipated, no cracks, perhaps in need of fresh paint. He moved through another doorway to the next room. It housed their spare refrigerator, a freezer, the furnace, and the well pump.

In the back was a third door. It was improvised from old barn wood, painted red, and hung crooked. Patrick affectionately called the room behind this door the dungeon. They rarely entered the space. He flipped the light switch. A fluorescent tube sputtered to life. In the very back, past the broken shelves loaded with books and camping gear, sat the boxes—his day's project. He counted twelve. Three uneven, four-high stacks with faded labels from the moving company, the bottom layers all crushed at odd angles, the corrugate strength fatigued from years of bearing the weight.

There was a musty smell, a dense dampness, and the silence of neglect. Patches of cobwebs tied the room together, their delicate structures in disrepair, loose filaments dancing to his movements. There were no windows and it was hard to see. Something metallic brushed across his head. A single incandescent bulb hung from a broken fixture. He pulled the chain and it lit the room. There was a sense of abandonment, cracks in the foundation peering from behind patches of blistered plaster, piles of plaster dust, a mechanical rowing machine, rusted barbells, a stained area rug reeking of cat pee. Even the spiders had moved on from this forgotten place.

He opened a box and saw it was filled with books: science fiction paperbacks he'd held onto since college. He looked in another, and another: all books, hardback novels, large tomes about business, history, and philosophy, some he'd read, all bought with good intentions, reflecting an obsessive interest, a burning excitement about new ideas, moments from the past, packed away, their power dissipated.

He arranged them on the floor to see what he wanted to keep. It didn't take long to realize he wanted to keep them all. He couldn't bear to get rid of any. He'd heard Helen's voice, and she wanted them out. Patrick wasn't sure what harm they were doing down here, out of sight.

When he touched the covers, read the titles, neurons flashed, memories appeared, unexpected shooting stars pulled him back. He wondered where these spirits had gone? When did they exit? When was the last time he felt excitement exploring a new unknown? Helen. Their life was supposed to be an adventure, a climb with no safety harness. Should we take the road less traveled? Screw the road had been their answer. Life got in the way. He recognized the danger in all of this, and he laid the books down, turned away from the awakened pain of these phantom limbs, once there, now gone, best forgotten.

He looked at the wall behind the stack of boxes. It was in bad shape, chunks of broken plaster on the floor. He probed it with one finger and a large piece fell and shattered. Unable to stop picking at it, another piece cracked off and dropped to the floor. He remembered the old axiom in the business world: 'When you're up to your ass in alligators, it's easy to forget that you came to drain the swamp.' This would be a slippery slope. Best leave it be, another job for another day. He stepped back and looked at the wall to make a final assessment. He noticed something. Through one of the larger cracks, he could see light.

Now he could not stop. He picked and scraped. Rather than finding foundation stones behind the plaster surface, he saw wood. His modest probes turned into a full-blown assault. He tore and pried at the wall. With the help of a tent peg, he hammered at it. The mess stirred up a cloud of dust, and he continued through a sneezing fit. He stood back to assess his progress and saw it: the outline of a door, hinges but no handle, full-sized, with light coming from behind. He pried at the door with the peg. It did not give. He forced harder; he braced a shoulder against the wall and his back muscles strained. He heard the wood creak, felt the tent peg start to bend, then came a snap, and the door dislodged.

Sweating now, he pulled the door open; leaning away, ready to run if some animal leapt out. Nothing did. He peered cautiously through the door, poking in just his head, catching his breath, letting his eyes adjust to the light, wondering what he had discovered. The air in the room smelled fresh, odorless, even reviving.

He looked down at the huge mess that crunched under his feet, but his concern was overcome by curiosity. He smiled at the thought of putting all the boxes of books in the room and sealing it back up. Helen would be happy and none the wiser, and, he'd have some comfort knowing they were there. He stuck his head in further and took a few steps, until he was through the door. The room was twice the size of the walk-in closet in their bedroom, empty, with a slight downward slope. He traced the tent peg across the dirt wall. He moved farther inside. He tightened his grip around the tent peg, extended his arm, and pointed into the room. Patrick remembered his son's obsession with fencing, and the many hours he spent watching his lessons at the YMCA. Patrick thought it was a beautiful, but useless skill. Now, he wished he had a foil—something longer.

As his eyes adjusted, he could see that the light was coming from yet another room, behind another wooden door. He estimated this was well out from under the house. An abandoned septic tank? But there was no odor. A root cellar that held generations-old treasures: ball jars of fruits and vegetables, salted meats, still freshly preserved? He remembered a friend found an old bomb shelter below his house—a remnant from the Cold War: a safe haven from a nuclear attack, packed with canned food, water, a propane tank, gas masks, and a Geiger counter. Patrick's concern dissolved, replaced by curiosity. The silence was total. He lowered his arm. Disarmed. The tent peg pointed at the floor. He moved in farther. The second door opened easily. The scene Patrick encountered was absurd. Even more peculiar was his acceptance of what he saw: some part of his subconscious took the sight for granted—oh, this.

The room was twice the size of the previous one; it was filled with bright light coming from no source he could identify. There were a few books neatly stacked along the dirt walls. At the far end was a large, ornate dining room chair. And in the chair, sitting rather formally was a man. The man looked up from the book he was reading and said, "Hello, Sir. I've been waiting for you. Waiting, for a long, long, time."

"For me?" Patrick pointed at himself with the tent peg. He seemed to forget that common sense would have him running back through the rooms, taking the cellar steps three at a time, and grabbing his cell phone to call the police.

The man stood up, and placed his book on the chair, then took a few intentional steps toward Patrick.

Feeling some rationality coming back, Patrick pointed the tent peg at the man. "Stop right there."

"No need for that," the man said as he continued his slow approach, reaching out, taking the tent peg from Patrick's hand.

"Who are you?" Patrick said.

"Damndest thing," the man said to himself, more than to Patrick. "I can't remember."

Patrick could now see him. The man was the same height as he was, same weight, had the same scar on his chin, and the same three-day beard, with gray flecks in the exact same spots.

"You're not dreaming," the man said, as though reading Patrick's thoughts. He was wearing farmer's clothes: flannel shirt, denim overalls, and work boots with the leather worn off the toes.

"How long have you been here?" Patrick asked.

"What year is it?" the man asked.

Patrick thought but could not remember. "What are you doing here? Why haven't we seen you, or heard you down here?" Patrick looked around; there were no visible doors or windows. "How do you get in and out?"

"Since I got in, I've never left."

"What about food and water?"

"I never get hungry or thirsty. I can't remember the last time I took a piss. Sometimes I can't remember when I took my last breath." The man's chest expanded as he pulled in air. He expelled it loudly through his mouth. His face had a hint of a smile.

"What have you been doing down here?"

"I sit and read. I wish I had more books. Read most of these more than once. Don Quixote has kept me good and occupied; I read that one twenty times. Proust helped pass the time. Not much of a story, but I would get lost in those pages. Moby Dick. I've got most of it memorized."

"I've never read any of those," Patrick said, feeling light-headed, his hands cold, Patrick started to wobble and almost fell over.

The man grabbed Patrick under the shoulder. "There now, take a load off." He settled him into the chair, pulled out the copy of Moby Dick from under Patrick and handed it to him. "That's better now, isn't it?"

Patrick felt restored. He shut his eyes and took in the cool air. It moved through his nostrils and traveled deep. Suffi-cient. He sat through many breaths. In silence. Thoughtless. He opened his eyes to find the man gone and the door shut. All the boxes he was to get rid of were neatly stacked along the dirt wall. He looked down at his shoes and noted he should get new ones as the leather was worn at the toes. He thought he heard noises outside the door, but his attention went to the book in his hand. He opened it to the first page and started to read.

HELEN CAME THROUGH THE DOOR, bent to one side from the weight of her laptop bag, which was overflowing with term papers. "Sorry I'm late," she said. "I tried to call and text you, but, as always, you never pickup." She shifted the bag to her other shoulder. "The faculty meeting went long, and I had to stay to catch up on grading papers. I still have a lot to do tonight." She was ready to pick a fight until she saw the dinner table.

Her husband stood there with one arm behind his back. "I hope you're hungry," he said. "I still need to finish cooking, but I've planned chicken cutlets, your mother's recipe, roasted potatoes, steamed asparagus, and a fresh green salad from the garden." He pulled a bouquet of wildflowers from behind his back and handed them to her.

She buried her face into the flowers and inhaled. Her eyes caught the meticulously set table with their bright red holiday china, half-full glasses of red wine, the flames of two lit candles flickered.

"I picked the flowers from your garden," he said, "got it weeded. Those boxes in the basement are gone. The wall back there was falling apart so I went to the hardware store and picked up some wire mesh, plaster and paint. It's good as new and won't be giving us any trouble. Also picked up the paint for the porches."

"You've had a productive day." Her need for an argument was gone.

"There's more." He took the flowers from her hands and replaced them with an envelope.

"What's this?"

"Take a look."

She opened the thick envelope and removed the papers. She saw plane tickets. "I don't get it?"

"I booked us tickets to Italy. Rented a villa on the southern coast for a month. We leave two weeks after your semester ends; I thought you might need some time to decompress. Maybe pick up some new clothes for the trip."

"What?" She was taken off-guard. "I mean this is great, but shouldn't we have discussed it? Can we afford it?"

"Decision is made," he said. "I figure we can't afford not to."

She looked at the table and the tickets, her laptop bag fell from her shoulder and hit the floor with a loud thunk. She clutched the envelope to her chest and laughed.

She took in her husband. Hands on his hips, feet spread a little wider than his shoulders, knees unlocked, as though prepared to stay upright if an unexpected swell shifted the ground beneath him. His eyes were clear and full of adventure. She felt his look touch her body. His lust.

She tried to connect the dots. "You shaved." She squinted; her heartbeat pulsed in her ears. Her lungs drew in an endless breath, a bright red flush spread across her skin. She tingled and wanted to scratch her arms. She exhaled and shook her head. "Who is this man that I'm looking at?"

With an impish grin, he answered, "Call me Ishmael."

PATRICK OPENED THE DOOR of the restaurant and held it for Helen and their friends, Larry and Beth. He followed them in.

"The place is not as busy as when we were here last month," Larry said. Their orders were taken. Larry gulped down a scotch, Helen and Beth sipped white wine, and Patrick shook the ice in his Rob Roy.

"So," Helen said, "Patrick has been very busy. He has some exciting news to tell you." All eyes at the table turned to Patrick, but he was distracted, his gaze fixed across the room. They turned to see what caught his attention and recognized the man at the bar from last month.

"Hey guys," Patrick said, as he stood up. "Excuse me for a minute. I see an old friend."

Frank's Used Books

Leo entered *Frank's Used Books*. The brass, vintage shop-keeper's bell, which hung precariously above the door, rang. Barry, Frank's business manager, sat behind the counter. This was unusual.

"Where's Frank?" Leo said.

"Frank died," Barry said.

"Oh my God. What happened?"

"He was one-hundred-and-three," Barry said.

Buying a book and having coffee with Frank had been Leo's Saturday ritual for the last sixteen years: a daughter dead from a drug overdose, a nasty divorce, two difficult job changes, three backbreaking moves, a stolen car, a stupid kitchen fire, fifteen traffic tickets, four presidential elections, a dead cat that he himself backed over, and, the weekly conversations with Frank about books and life.

Barry lifted a shoebox from under the counter. It was filled with envelopes. He rifled through them, retrieved one, and handed it to Leo. It was addressed to Leo with Frank's distinctive, shaky handwriting.

"He has one of these for all his regulars," Barry said. "Frank wanted me to tell everyone to open them at home. Alone."

"He prepared these? Did he know he was going to die?" Leo asked.

"He was one-hundred-and-three." Barry said.

Leo remembered discussing death with Frank. Leo asked Frank if he thought a person's life flashed before his eyes at the moment of death. Frank's face formed a sly grin, and he said, "That happens to *me* every day."

"You've never read Salinger," Frank told Leo the first time they met. He had asked him for a suggestion. "Well," Frank said, "start with *Nine Stories*, I think it's his best work." That is how it went, every week, for sixteen years. Frank would recommend a book to Leo and tell him to come back *only* when he'd finished it. "Hold off on *Ulysses* and start your Joyce journey with *Dubliners*."

Leo made it a point to finish the book within the week so he could sit with Frank. He never missed a Saturday.

Flannery O'Connor, Raymond Carver, Pynchon, Camus, Toni Morrison. Ray Bradbury, Dostoevsky, Harlan Ellison, Isabel Allende, and Hemingway, all of them introduced to Leo by Frank, among many, many others.

"If you read only one book by Stephen King," Frank said, "it should be his first collection: *Night Shift*. Also, *The Lottery and Other Stories* by Shirley Jackson is a must; she has quite a range." They drank coffee and talked about each book for an hour. "Of course, Charles Johnson's *Middle Passage* is great, an award winner, but *Oxherding Tale* is where you should start."

Leo once took a week off from work to finish *Don Quixote*. He did not want to miss his Saturday with Frank.

He turned the envelope in his hands. "At least the store will preserve his legacy," Leo said to Barry.

"He left everything to me," Barry said. "I'm shutting it down, selling the building and all, taking the money to travel Europe for the next two years. A bucket list dream."

"Two years?" Frank said, "Then what?"

Barry smiled and shrugged.

THE ENVELOPE SAT ON Leo's mantle unopened for twenty years. He felt not having closure with Frank would keep Frank alive.

Leo's son found it while he and his wife were cleaning out Leo's house. He opened it.

"Bonnie, look at this," Leo's son said. He read aloud. "Leo, Time has an end. This is yours." Leo's son looked at his wife and spoke the date shakily written on the note. "Was this when my dad died?"

"Maybe," Bonnie said, "The coroner thought his body sat in bed for as much as two weeks before his neighbor called about the smell."

He looked at the note. "Who's Frank?"

"No idea," she said. "Do you want to get back to work by Monday, or is every piece of trash going to take you an hour to analyze?"

"What about all his books," Leo's son said. "There must be a thousand."

"Bag 'em all up, and throw them in the dumpster," she said.

Leo's son found *Ficciones* by Jorge Luis Borges. He slipped the paperback into his back pocket: a little something to remember his father.

Darshan Renovations

Harold's feet lost the ladder. His fingers wrapped around the roof gutter, at a seam. Under his weight the metal split. Moist gutter crud dripped onto his face, into his mouth. He fell, spitting out dirt. The ground greeted Harold with no forgiveness: pain jolted his heels, his butt, and then his head smacked the blacktop driveway. When he came to, everything hurt. "Tie off the ladder," his wife had told him. "Tie it off so you don't slip and crack your skull." He waited for his body to reveal what was broken.

Newton scurried over and licked his face. Harold rolled away from Newton and propped up on an elbow. Newton climbed over, straddled him, and continued to lash with her tongue. Harold sat up and grabbed the dog's head to push him away. Both the dog's ears were covered in blood. "My God," Harold said. He guessed the ladder had hit Newton and cracked her skull. She bled from both ears. *Tie off the ladder.*

Harold stood, picked up Newton. Hugged him. He lifted an ear and looked in. The canal was dry, clean. He stroked the full length of his body. It was streaked with blood. Newton struggled free, got down, and started to lick the gutter crud. Harold reached to grab Newton and saw blood drip from his hand. He inspected his palm, flexed back his fingers, a gash opened. He clenched his fist shut. Same wound on his other hand. He squeezed both hands tight. Blood dribbled to the ground. Harold leaned forward and puked. Breakfast: French toast, re-heated corned beef hash, two English muffins, and a leftover piece of blueberry pie with whipped cream. Newton looked up from the gutter crud, sniffed the ground, zig-zagged his way to the breakfast puddle. The dog licked greedily.

Three hours after the fall, Larry, the mailman, rang Harold's doorbell, and let himself in. Newton ran up, wagged his tail, and waited for a treat. Larry gave him the usual bacon-flavored biscuit, knelt down, and let Newton lick his face. He stood and laid the mail on the kitchen counter.

"How old is she now? Two years?" Larry said.

"Almost three," Harold said. "Gwen passed in May. It'll be three years."

"What happened to your gutter?"

"I went up to clean it, slipped, and ripped it down." Harold held up his bandaged hands.

"Looks bad," Larry said. "What hospital did you go to? Those bandages look like crap."

"Did it myself."

"You're lucky you didn't break your neck." Larry shook his head. "Going to Mass tomorrow night?"

"Yes," Harold said. This was one of the promises he made to Gwen before she died. Harold abided. He was bitter with God, and let him know it every week.

"That foreign priest is visiting," Larry said. "The one from Argentina. With stigmata. You'll fit right in." Larry looked at his watch. "They're busing in sick folks from all over the state, in hopes of a miracle. Maybe he'll take care of those hands."

"Ha, ha," Harold said.

"Seriously though, you should bring in Newton."

"I don't think God heals dogs."

"You never know," Larry said. "Gotta go. Hey, the gutter, you're too old to do house maintenance. Just hire somebody."

"Yeah. Too cheap I guess," Harold said. "I've got the time." Harold liked Larry's daily visits. He'd always pop in, even if the mail fit in the box; even if there was no mail at all. Gwen said the Lord never blessed them with children so she could pour all that love into her students. Gwen taught Larry's youngest and got to know him and his wife real well. Their girl was dyslexic. Gwen gave her extra attention, strategies and skills with which to do well in school. After Gwen died, Larry stayed close to Harold.

Harold cleaned up the driveway. Swept the gutter crud into a pile, scooped it up and put it in the garden. It was a bit of a magic trick for him. Leaves fall into the gutter, clog things up, soak in the rain and *ta da*—the best soil in the world. This was a business proposition for someone who was still interested in making his mark in the world.

That night Newton sat in her usual spot in the living room: Harold's lap. With his bandaged hands, he smoothed her fur, kissed her, looked into her blind eyes and felt guilt. It was his fault and no one knew but him and her.

Harold thought about that day three years ago when Gwen walked in the door with an eight-week-old puppy, just weaned. "She's a purebred Weimaraner."

"No, no, no," Harold said.

"Honey," Gwen said, "I'm worried about you all alone every day. You need a companion." She set the puppy on the floor of their kitchen. She sniffed at the ground, squatted and peed. "She needs to be housebroken."

"No shit," Harold said. "What about travel? What do we do with her then?"

"That," Gwen said, "Is off a ways. We'll figure something out."

"Got a name?"

"No," Gwen said. "That's your first job."

Harold took to training her with a spray bottle they used for their houseplants. When she had an accident, a few squirts in the face, then out the door. He tired of this routine after a few days. He walked into the living room to find the puppy shitting on their new carpet, and went ballistic. Screaming, he grabbed the dog by its collar, lifted it off the ground, grabbed the spray bottle and let loose point blank into the dog's face. The dog screamed. Harold thought it sounded like a human baby. He threw her out the door, watched her rub her face on the lawn, scrape at her eyes with her paws. Then he smelled the bleach. He had grabbed a spray bottle of bleach.

Harold lied to Gwen, and the vet. Told them he was cleaning the toilet and somehow the pup got into the bleach. The vet said her eyes were badly damaged, but she might get some sight back. It was Gwen's idea to call her Newton, after John Newton who wrote the gospel song, "Amazing Grace." *I was lost, but now I'm found, I was blind but now I see. There's always hope*, she said.

They sat together a night after the vet visit, and that's when Gwen told Harold about her visit to the doctor for back pain. It was cancer. Ovarian. Stage four. Metastised to several other organs. She had known for a month, and was told she had less than a year left. It turned out to be weeks.

THE EVENING AFTER Gwen's funeral, Newton sat in Harold's lap. He rocked her in his favorite chair on the back porch. The sunset was beautiful, one of those nights when fat contrails decorated the sky in all directions, and distant clouds looked like islands. He leaned over and kissed her and told her he loved her. He told her she was his little girl. "Are you my little girl?" he said. "Yes you are…yes you are." He kissed the top of her head. He rubbed his nose against her soft ear. She looked at him, and all Harold could see was the burn scars on her eyes. Eyes that did not blame. Harold would no longer notice her eyes; he could not forgive himself, but, perhaps, forget.

Weeks after Gwen's death, Harold's doctor suggested medication, something mild to offset the grief, help keep him balanced. "I haven't cried," Harold told his doctor. That's not good, the doctor answered; do you have someone to talk to? To confide in? Harold shook his head and thought of Newton. Harold decided not to pick up the prescription. He decided to chop wood. A full cord was stacked against the side of the garage—three week's work.

Leaves fell from the trees and the air was crisp. An airplane engine sounded overhead, a small plane, a single-engine prop. Newton lifted her head from his lap. Startled. She looked up. He calmed her down. "Just a plane," he said. "Just a plane." She laid her head back down.

They'd been planning to travel. Two more years teaching and Gwen would follow him into retirement: full pension, social security and Medicare. They would check off all the usual places: Paris, Venice, Costa Rica, but they also wanted to walk the Great Wall, learn to Tango in Buenos Aires, get lost for a month in Spain, and his favorite: the Hotel Kakslauttanen in Finland, where they would stay in a glass igloo and make love under the eternal Northern Lights.

He held her hand in the hospital. "Take care of Newton, go to all those places we never got to, and go to Mass every week."

"I promise," Harold said.

Both his knees cracked, as he got up from the porch chair. He set his little girl down. She was tired and melted from his arms onto the floor. There was a day when he could carry her in, but now, she was pushing seventy pounds. He had to get out of the suit. One more look at the sky. He decided to make the first fire of the season that night.

He hung the suit in his closet, but before shutting the door he reached into the pocket and slid out the papers and holy card. It was one of their little games. To try and guess the last time he wore it: was it a funeral or a wedding? It was a funeral. Hers. He looked at her name on the card: Gwendolyn Gibbs.

HAROLD TRIED TO OPEN the car door but could not get out.

"Hang on," Larry said. "New car, it automatically locks." He pushed a button. "Try now."

"No," Harold said.

"Now?"

The car door opened. "Got it," Harold said. St. Mary's church was one of the oldest parishes, and buildings, in the area, built in 1874 by Irish Catholic settlers who started the parish in 1859. Three months previous, the Vatican declared Father Cathan O'Connell a saint. He was one of the original pastors at the church. The three miracles all involved miraculous healings. He was said to have lived up to his name, which meant battle in the old language. He fought off many a Protestant gang and single-handedly saved the church from being burnt down. This is why St. Mary's was chosen to be one of the churches on the tour of Father Santiago Moreno. Father Moreno was blessed with stigmata and was on a world tour.

Father Moreno told the faithful that while fasting in the Argentinian mountains in Catamarca, he was visited by an angel who identified himself as St. Francis of Assisi, and instructed him to preach peace to the world.

"Do you know that St. Francis of Assisi was the first documented case of stigmata back around 1200?" Larry said. They walked to the back of the line leading into the church. "Just like Father Moreno: both hands, both feet, and his side."

"I did hear that," Harold said.

"He's been healing people all over the world. I saw a man get up out of a wheelchair on TV. Then the guy raised his hands and had stigmata himself. Temporary they said, as a sign of transference of power."

Harold looked at his bandaged hands, tried to put them in his pockets, but with the bulky wrap, they would not fit.

"He's been verified by a Vatican doctor. He travels with three doctors and two bodyguards," Larry said.

"Bodyguards?"

"Sure. The Vatican is rich. Father Moreno, a living saint, would be worth a nice ransom."

They stood in line. A priest with a thick accent walked past them as he announced, "Please be brief. Father Moreno is weak today. Just a brief stop for a blessing. Do not touch Father Moreno." The priest looked down at Harold's hands and frowned.

"You see that look he gave you?" Larry said.

"Yeah, what's with that?"

"I think your hands," Larry said.

An hour later, it was their turn to see the stigmata priest. Incense escaped from the holes of a gold thurible. An altar boy held it, giving its chains a brief swing as each person passed. Father Moreno sat in a chair that looked like an old throne. He was immense. Fat. Unshaved. Bald. A black robe covered his girth. His hands and bare feet were wrapped with white bandages, tainted with red spots, the blood that seeped through. The wound under his ribs, the place where the soldiers thrust a spear in Christ's side, was not visible. He had a broad smile on his face. Two large priests flanked him. Americans. The type of guys you'd expect to see outside an exclusive, big-city dance club.

Larry stopped, faced Father Moreno, got onto one knee, and bowed his head. The priest made the sign of the cross with one hand and mumbled a blessing. One of the big priests leaned over, put a hand under Larry's arm and directed him to move on.

Harold leaned down. The Argentinian priest lunged towards Harold, and grabbed his hands so fast both his bodyguards moved to Harold. Father Moreno pulled Harold to him and looked at his bandaged hands. He nodded vig-orously. He spoke to Harold. "*Bendice a tu perro que el diablo se haya ido de tu vida,*" the priest said. "*Arreglar la casa e ir en paz.*"

One of the bodyguards, who stood a number of feet away, moved between them, grabbed Harold by the shoulders and pushed him past the priest, up the hall, and out the door.

"What the heck did I do?" Harold asked.

"This is not a joke," the bodyguard priest said. "You come in here with those bandages, making fun of Father Moreno… he called you a dog, a devil. Told you to go." He stopped and poked Harold in the chest with one meaty finger. "Get out."

"That's not what he…I'm not making fun of him," Harold said. "I'm cut on both hands." With that, the big priest grabbed Harold by the wrist and unwrapped the makeshift bandages from Harold's right hand. There was no wound. Harold looked at this and took the bandage off his left hand. No wound. "This is a miracle," Harold said.

"Get out," the priest said. He pushed Harold in the back.

Harold sat in the car with Larry. "What did Father Moreno say to you?" Larry stared at Harold's hands. "How bad were the cuts?"

"Real bad. Stitches bad. Now they're gone," Harold ignored Larry's first question, although he had heard what the stigmata priest said to him. *Bless your dog, the devil is gone from your life. Fix the house and go in peace.* He had no idea what it meant.

"Pretty cool." Larry started the car. "I felt warm when he blessed me." He made a circle with his arm. "But my shoulder still hurts."

"From carrying a bag?" Harold said.

"No. I don't walk on my route. I thought you knew that," Larry said. "It's the god-darned Amazon Prime houses, everywhere. Used to just be mail. Now it's all these boxes. The Beckers have a case of tonic water delivered, twice a week."

Larry inched the car forward. People were still arriving. A few wheelchairs. "That's a lot of gin and tonics."

"You know what's in the boxes?"

"Sure," Larry said. "I had a friend who was a radio DJ, and he could pick up a CD case and tell you if there was a disc in there, or not. Try that sometime. Carriers can tell you what's in every box; almost tell you the color of the item. It's a sixth sense you develop over time. I think we all have it in one way or another. Seeing things others can't."

Harold waved goodbye to Larry as he drove off. He opened his front door. Newton jumped on him: her usual greeting after being alone. When Gwen was alive they tried to train this out of the pup, but Harold liked the attention. Glad that someone was happy to see him. He let her out and they walked the path through the woods on the back of his property. The moon was full, the sky clear. Harold never tired of the silhouette of the old barn, the house, and the other outbuildings that made up his property.

He rubbed his hands together. A miracle? He wasn't sure. Perhaps the cuts hadn't been as bad as he thought. But all that blood? No, they *were* bad. This *was* a miracle. He didn't feel anything. No elation, surprise, no need to shout that God was alive and working in the world. He felt guilt. A wasted miracle. Are there just so many to go around? Were these cuts worth the gift? Now if Gwen were here, that would be something to shout about. But she wasn't.

He whistled and Newton came to his side. Harold reached down and patted her on the head. There was something when the priest looked at him, into him, and saw everything. He knew about the bleach; Harold was sure of this. That must be why he mentioned the dog. Was I forgiven? Newton bolted ahead. Harold called her and cringed, for he had seen her run into one too many trees.

Fix the house? Harold knew the priest got that one wrong. Harold and Gwen dreamt of owning a small farm when they were first married. But the proposition was too expensive outside the city. Fifteen years later and a transfer across the country got them closer. Then Gwen set her heart on their current place: a completely renovated farmhouse, four outbuildings, an impressive red barn, ten mostly wooded acres. The neighbors said the owners would never sell; they spent seven years completely renovating the place. Gwen told Harold she almost drove off the road when she saw an open house sign in the front yard. Harold said "No, no way." Gwen said, "Let's just look at it so I know why we won't want to live there." This seemed harmless to Harold, as harmless at just going to look at a puppy.

The house was perfect. All their furniture fit as though the place was waiting for it. They would not have to do anything, not even paint one room. Twenty years later it needed a new roof, furnace, septic system, well pump, water heater, washer, dryer, and dishwasher. The back deck had to be taken down and rebuilt. The whole electrical system had to be upgraded to match code. They did everything, rationalizing that these structural improvements would be a good investment in the property. Now, Harold could not think of a single thing that needed to be fixed. The priest got that one wrong.

He walked Newton back to the house and felt that a weight had been lifted. Newton's eyes. Harold felt at peace with it. Did the priest absolve him of this sin? He thought yes.

Harold was chopping wood, sweating, when Larry drove up in his mail truck. Harold never got used to the steering wheel being on the wrong side. It looked odd. Larry stepped out and Newton ran up to greet him. He made her sit, dangled a treat over her head, bent over and she licked his face, their usual ritual.

"Hey, what's with her eyes?" Larry said. He gave her the treat.

Harold stopped the axe mid-swing and felt a pang of guilt. He wasn't as faithful with her eye drops over the past few weeks. Her conjunctivitis must be back: bloodshot, maybe the white goo.

Harold put the axe down, ready for a breather.

"They look great," Larry said.

Larry knelt down and held Newton from behind. Harold looked into her eyes. The scars were gone. Her eyes were clear, the irises were amber, almost gold.

"I thought they would be blue. Aren't a Weimaraner's eyes blue?" Larry said.

"Only as a puppy." Harold remembered those blue puppy eyes. Striking.

"Do you think this is the priest?"

"No," Harold said. "No. Just time and her meds."

Harold took the file box from the top shelf in the first floor bedroom closet, and carried it into the kitchen. He set up his bills on auto-pay after his wife died. He never filed anything anymore. He never filed anything when she was alive; this was a task she managed. He popped open the black plastic box, and looked for a file folder that would have the info on the dog ophthalmologist that treated Newton. The vet told him her eyes might get better, but could also get worse. He had the eye drops to give her, and was only supposed to come back if he noticed any changes. That was several years ago. Now, there were changes.

After flipping through a few folders, he realized he'd grabbed the wrong box. The manila folders were all labeled, and filled with manuals and receipts for home purchases: the well, the roof, other appliances. When Harold saw the thick file in the back of the box, his heart sank. The word *bathroom* triggered a Pandora's box of many fights with Gwen. Newton started to whine.

The dog looked out the kitchen door that led to the deck. Harold also looked. The birdfeeder. Two bright red cardinals were on the birdfeeder. Newton could see them. This was a new development.

Harold opened the bathroom folder. He handled the pages with reverence, delicate turns of each sheet, care taken not to get things out of order. The overall outline, pictures of their current bathroom, pages torn from magazines of double vanities, mirrors, light fixtures, tile designs, bathtubs, at the end was a PowerPoint presentation for a prospective contractor to give an estimate. It consumed him for two hours. He thought of burning it, but could not. He knew it would be a sacrilegious act, to desecrate this holy book. He could see how Gwen's mind worked.

The next day he showed it to Larry.

"Do you have a leak or something?" Larry said.

Harold shook his head. "Gwen wanted this, but we just put on a new roof, the heater…seemed like a waste of money."

"Yeah, I thought you wanted to travel. Who cares about a room where you spend fifteen minutes a day to shit, shave, and shower."

"Exactly what I said." Harold looked up in the direction of the bathroom. "She said…" Harold couldn't finish. Tears welled up in his eyes. He bit his lip.

"You okay?" Larry asked.

Harold held up a hand, to indicate he needed a moment. He remembered how they fought about this bathroom. The sleepless night in bed when Gwen whispered, "I just want a nice place to take a bath."

Harold pictured her in the new bathroom, renovated to her specifications. He could bring it to life from the details in the folder. Warm, clean, candlelit, a book, a glass of wine, the thick smell of lilacs, Gwen's relaxed smile, a deep sigh of satisfaction as she sank into the deep tub. Then he saw her in her coffin. He tried to block the memory. Harold burst into tears.

Larry gave Harold a hug. Newton wagged her tail and jumped up on them. "George. My wife's brother," Larry said.

"He could do it." Newton looked at Harold and Larry, her pupils constricted, then dilated. She had beautiful amber eyes.

George was a big guy, strong, dark short hair, a well-trimmed gray beard. "The cost is going to vary depending on what you pick for the fixtures," George said. "The tile alone can go from fifty-eight cents a square foot up to thirteen dollars."

They talked through options and Harold insisted on the best, of everything. George suggested underfloor heating, removing a wall to open up the space, and floor tile with a wood look to add texture and warmth to the room. He spent thirty minutes working on the estimate, punctuated with calls to suppliers. Harold remembered yelling at his wife that *we will never spend fifteen thousand dollars on a fucking bathroom!* Although George only asked for half up front, Harold wrote him a check for the full amount: $27,000.

As a favor, George squeezed in the job ahead of some others. After the hardware arrived he completed it in less than two weeks. Harold inspected it. The room was cleaner than he ever imagined. The dated green tub and sinks were replaced with striking beige fixtures. The tiles on the shower wall and floor complimented each other and tied the room together. All walls were straight. The ceiling was fixed. The rusted heater vents were removed. It felt bigger, smelled fresh. "I rerouted the piping, it was old. You won't have clogs anymore," George said.

"This is beautiful."

"Your wife did this. Her plans were so detailed. Well thought out." George took a handkerchief from his back pocket and wiped a small smudge off the mirror. "Do you mind if I take some pictures and use them in my portfolio?"

"Fine with me," Harold said. "Do you have a few minutes? I want to show you something." They met and talked in the kitchen for two hours.

The next day, Larry appeared at eleven-thirty, his usual time. He gave a treat to Newton. "George said it turned out great."

"Yes. Remarkable." Harold said. "Thank you. I wish Gwen had met him."

"George said the same thing, thought they could have worked together." Larry leaned over and pulled up a sock. Even though it was only in the forties, he wore his uniform shorts. "How is it? To use."

"Don't know," Harold said. "I can't bring myself to spoiling it. Been using the first floor bathroom. Now with the other work I'm staying downstairs."

"George told me about that. The other work." Larry took a breath, paused and decided not to say anything. He saw a large book in Harold's hand. "What are you reading?"

"*Don Quixote*," Harold said.

"It's a big one," Larry said.

"Yep," Harold said. "Something to keep me occupied while all this work is going on."

After the work started on the bathroom, Harold put the file box back in the closet, and took down another to find the name of Newton's vet. That box was filled with folders similar to the one for the bathroom: overall outline of the work, estimates, pictures, and a PowerPoint presentation. There was one file for every room in the house: the three upstairs bedrooms, including building over the open space in the garage to create a master bedroom with huge closets and a whirlpool tub. The dining room, first floor bedroom, family room, and the kitchen, all had folders. The basement had plans for workout equipment and a sauna. Even the little laundry room on the first floor, with its cramped toilet, had new plans to expand into a walk-in pantry. Rugs were to be replaced with hardwood floors, closets expanded, custom cabinets, new furniture and appliances, coordinated color schemes. No detail was left untouched.

"I decided to freshen the whole place up," Harold said. "For Gwen."

Larry's mind filled with images of the Taj Mahal, tombs in the pyramids. Harold knew: he was trying to make up for what he withheld from his wife when she was alive. Perhaps this was a waste of money, a real mental illness of some sort that Harold should get checked out. He pulled up his other sock. "I think she would…" he paused, not sure how to complete the thought.

Harold waited, nodded, and turned away.

When each room was complete, Harold inspected it… and shut the door. He offered George a 10% premium to bump up ahead of other clients. In the middle of the next summer, George was working on the last room: the basement. Harold continued not to use each room after it was completed, backing up to smaller and smaller portions of the house. Cornered, but not like a rat. As each room was complete, more of the house created in the image Gwen had for it, Harold felt something grow inside of him: a release.

He cooked on a gas grill in the yard that was next to the tent. It was a Spartan space: an air mattress and sleeping bag, a cooler, a lantern, a well-organized stack of clothes, a small table with a picture of his wife and a pen and pad, and Newton's bed. Twenty feet from the tent was a porta-potty. He stopped shaving and bathing.

Larry drove up. Worried about his friend, he had called city services. They were familiar with the property, since they had come by to issue permits, approve electrical and gas upgrades to the house. There was nothing they could do, or felt they should do. The new assessment on the house would be a nice boost to the small township's property tax coffers, and raise the value of the surrounding homes.

Harold offered Larry a cup of coffee. He accepted. "I have a favor to ask you," Harold said.

"Sure, anything." Newton's head rested on Harold's feet. She snored.

"I found a paper with a list of places in the states." Harold took it from his chest pocket, unfolded it, and gave it to Larry. It was a woman's handwriting. Gwen, he guessed. Larry recognized some of the names on the list: Grand Canyon, Niagara Falls, and Devil's Tower. Others he had no idea about: Cadillac Ranch, The House on the Rock, Lake Shasta Caverns. The list covered both sides of the paper.

"Quite a list," Larry said. He handed the paper back to Harold.

"We always discussed travelling abroad," Harold said. "She made me promise to go to the places we talked about. I could never take Newton overseas. Now I would never be able to leave her." The dog lifted its head, looked up, and laid it back down. "But these are…we could drive."

Larry looked at his watch. "Shoot, Harold, I'm a bit behind and have to run. See you tomorrow." He gulped down his coffee and left. Three houses later he realized he'd rushed off before Harold had a chance to ask him the favor.

For a full week, Larry stopped by, but Harold was not there. He even popped in more than once, but no Harold. When he called him, it went right to voicemail. Then, one day, Larry was relieved to see Harold sitting on the front steps with Newton. The tent and porta-potty were gone. "So you finally moved back in," Larry said.

"No. But it's all done," Harold said. He pointed across the property. Larry saw a large truck with a sleep-in camper on top.

"What's that?"

"That's our Rocinante." Harold scratched Newton's head.

"Is that a camper brand?" Larry said.

"Never mind," Harold laughed. "The favor."

"I'm so sorry, I left in a rush," Larry said.

"Could you put a hold on my mail?" Harold explained he was going on a trip for a few months, maybe a year, to visit all the places on Gwen's list.

"Postal service doesn't do it for that long," Larry said. "How 'bout, I collect your mail and keep it in a box for when you get back…not as your mail carrier, just as a friend."

"That would be great." Harold assured him that everything else was taken care of. Lawn cutting, snow plowing, lights on timers, even scheduled a guy to clean the gutters in the spring. Nothing could go wrong with the house, it was all new.

"Maybe get me a key before you go, just in case," Larry said.

"We leave now, right after you do," Harold said. He pulled out a carabiner keychain holding a leather bird ornament and two keys. "These are for the top and bottom locks. You have my cell number."

Larry took the keychain; it was lighter than he'd expected it to feel. He hugged Harold, patted him on the back.

A quarter mile down the road, Larry realized in all the years he'd known Harold that was the first time he'd hugged him. There was just the somber handshake at Gwen's funeral.

Larry wished he'd spent more time with Harold. It was as though he didn't really know him. He knew facts and some stories, but he didn't really know him. This bothered Larry, he vowed to never let it happen again, with anyone in his life. But that feeling faded. After a few months, when he drove by, he never even looked over at Harold's house.

EIGHT MONTHS AFTER Harold left on the trip, was the first time Larry felt compelled to call him. It was about the Church. There had been nothing, no contact, since Harold drove off. Larry was excited. He practiced what he was going to say. Very fast: *Harold it's Larry—nothing's wrong. No problems, just wanted to tell you some news. How are you doing? How's Newton? Did you see the Grand Canyon?*

He wanted to tell him that Father Moreno had disappeared in Argentina. There was some rumor of kidnapping, but the church said that the stigmata priest simply left the earth and ascended into heaven. The Vatican started a canonization process. He would be Saint Santiago. Only the third Argentinian Saint.

Larry sat in his car, parked in front of Harold's house. He opened a can of soda. He didn't realize how much he missed him. He wondered when he was coming back. He dialed Harold's number.

"I'm sorry the number you reached is no longer in service, please check the number and try again." Larry did, three times. He called the phone company, and all they could tell him was that the number was no longer in service, and there was no forwarding number.

Larry got out of the car. He felt regret for something, for everything: the boxes of Harold's mail, the unused house, and his underdeveloped friendship with him. He feared he might never see Harold again.

Larry had never seen the inside of Harold's house after the renovations, and decided to peek into the windows. He went up on the front porch. The shades masked any view of the interior. He took out the keychain, but the keys Harold had given him did not work on the locks. Larry went to the back of the house: the keys didn't open the back door either.

He looked at the keys and the ornament hanging from the carabiner. He wondered, did Harold make a mistake? Or did he do this on purpose?

Larry looked at the house Harold had given him charge over: an impenetrable island.

An ominous sound filled the sky. An uneven chorus of one syllable honks. Larry looked up and saw wave after wave of geese migrating in *V* formations. Hundreds of birds, he thought, thousands. An endless stream.

Larry watched the geese and felt a tug, similar to the time he looked over Niagara Falls and had to fight off the urge to jump, to float down, to fly in the cool mist. Now, he was being pulled up, to migrate, to ascend, and to be carried beyond this place. Larry was unnerved. Where was Harold? Or Father Moreno? Was all the magic in the world moving on without him?

He shut his eyes, listened to the bird's infinite chant, took a deep breath, and could smell in the air that it was about to rain.

The Samadhi Tones

Justin Langbecker opened his eyes. The hospital bed beneath him *buzzed* as his body was tilted into an upright position. He tried to lift his hands, but their straps secured them to the bed's side rails. He desperately tried to break free.

"Whoa! Whoa! Whoa! Settle down, King Kong." Justin's eldest brother leaned in and grabbed Justin's forearms, firmly, but with care not to disturb the IV tubes. His youngest sister gently pushed his forehead back onto the pillow.

"Where am I?" Justin said.

All ten of his siblings traveled from around the country to be by his side. Justin looked at each of their faces and laughed to himself as he thought, *well, I'm not dead: half of them would be in Heaven, the other half in Hell.*

"Is Mom here?" Justin said. His siblings traded glances, tried to read each other's minds to agree on a response.

In the back of the room, two sisters and a brother, started to argue.

"Shut up, for Christ's sake," his older sister said to the three arguers.

"Watch your language!" his youngest sister said.

A middle brother yanked a vape pen from his twin's hand, "You can't do that in here! Are you stupid?"

"I brought you fresh cut flowers from my garden," his middle sister said. She thrust the bouquet into Justin's face. He flinched.

Justin sneezed. Sneezed again, and again. He coughed. Coughed again, harder. He couldn't stop. Pain flashed through his torso. The contractions of his chest muscles *click*ed. The wires holding his sternum together loosened. His siblings saw blood spread through his shirt. They called for help. Justin was sedated. Under heavy eyelids, Justin remembered the last time he saw his mother; the words he yelled at her. He went to sleep.

ONE DAY LATER, Justin woke up, restored for the second time. His arms moved unrestricted when he raised them to rub his eyes. In the corner of the room, his ninety-two-year-old mother was seated in a chair.

"I'm thirsty," Justin said.

His mother stood and brought Justin a cup with a straw. She moved it to his mouth and he sipped.

"Ginger ale," Justin said.

"Your favorite," his mother said. She beamed. "I remember."

She set down the drink and placed something in Justin's hands. His fingers made contact, and Justin remembered. A smile crept across his face. He tilted the toy in different directions. The sound, like tiny wind chimes, brought him a deep joy. Justin thought he could live the rest of his life, whether days, weeks, years, or decades, right there, gently rolling the sublime toy back and forth, back and forth.

"Happy Apple," Justin said. "*My* Happy Apple."

"I always kept it," his mother said. "I got rid of everything after your father died, and all you kids moved out." She sighed. "But not this, the sound transports me back..."

Justin looked away from the red, plastic apple with big eyes and an innocent smile. "What I said to you the last time we spoke..."

"Shush," his mother said. "That was thirty-two years ago."

"I was angry," Justin said. He searched his memory for the emotional fulcrum, but failed to retrieve it. "Angry at everything," he surrendered.

"You know," his mother said, "those tones are based on Balinese Gamelan musical instruments." She looked at her son. "I see you, a baby, holding it. I hear your carefree giggle."

"Where's…the gang?"

"I sent them away." She smiled. "The good news is that they were all here to help. The bad news is that they were all here to help."

Justin and his mother laughed.

She moved closer to him. "I don't know how much time either one of us has left," she said. "We can't fill in a thirty-two year hole, but we can be here now. If you want."

He nodded. "I'm here Mom." His hands cradled the toy…a sacred relic.

She kissed the top of his head, pressed her cheek against his face, and surrounded his hands with hers; the gentle motion, the music from the chimes: their sacrament.

They could live the rest of their lives, whether days, weeks, years, or decades, right there, gently rolling the sublime toy back and forth, back and forth, back and forth, back and forth…

The Pathology of Love

Gloria Stiles stretched her left leg and her knee popped. She liked the sound of her torn meniscus. It reminded her she was not a victim, but in control: imperfect by choice, the music of the sound, her composition, a little rebellion she could call her own.

Her index finger rested on the keyboard's enter key. Just a bit of pressure and she would cause havoc: slam the controls forward, take the world's smooth glide path into an out of control descent. With her other hand she poked chopsticks into a bowl and grabbed a large portion of sliced onions, marinated in vinegar and soy sauce, an addiction from her childhood in Seoul. A quick shake and then she shoved them into her mouth. She savored their bittersweet bite.

She no longer wanted her father's help. "You can't waste your time studying art," he would say. "Science, business, you need to make money. Go for art, and I'll cut you off. A starving artist."

As always, she gave in. She remembered the saying that parents first give children life, and then try to give them theirs, or what they wished theirs had been. Gloria wanted her own path. She needed a way to escape.

Gloria loved Seoul. She missed it. How easy it was to be anonymous there, even for an American girl with a famous father. An enchanted and chaotic place, where the poetic pragmatism of clustered high rises finds sanctuary in the steadfast gaze of distant mountains. Urban rush balanced by Buddhist temple still. Crowds bleed to the streets from subway stations, Seoul's circulatory system feeding the extensive metropolis above, and the heap of stores below. Coffee shop after coffee shop. Packed restaurants, the smell of pork and beef barbecue, fried chicken, steamed dumplings, the din of exultant talk amplified by too much beer and soju. Young girls walked arm-in-arm, dressed alike: twinsies. Professional men in sharp suits strode with purpose, and the elderly decorated with expensive hiking attire meandered in colorful flocks. These recollections of hers were of a time before the bio-tech revolution. She thought about going back to visit, but preferred to let the past, her past, still have the breath of artificial life.

And there was Mr. Yun, her after-school tutor and mentor, who'd taught her how to draw with pencils, took her on adventures to explore the city under the city, showed her the best vendors for dumplings and squid. She missed the ache in her legs from the long hikes to Ongnyeobong Peak to look at Seoul from the eyes of God, watch the old men reward their accomplishment with cups of white makgeolli, and hear Mr. Yun lecture on world history.

She caught onto his programming lessons and learned to code like a college grad. In the air, she envisioned the zeroes and ones that mimicked small strokes of Mr. Yun's pencils: invisible textures that deceived the eye.

"See," he said, "four strokes of the pen, and the bird changes from flat to alive, ready to fly off the page." He picked up another pencil, placed it in her hand, and arranged her fingers. "Not too tight, not too loose. Don't think, let it flow from here." He touched her solar plexus. "Anahata… heart chakra."

She practiced with pencils, but nothing she drew looked real. Her computer code was her art. Her buildings and birds sat lifeless and misshaped on the page, but with her machine language, she gave life to worms that slipped through firewalls, distributed processes that hid resource usage, all masked in rootkits.

Yun tapped the screen. "How did you do that?"

"With this," Gloria said, a finger to her chest. "Evil hidden in beauty."

"The Buddhist monks, the old ones, who practiced *Bool-kyo Musol,* used to fight great battles." Yun squinted at the screen, searched it. "A mere ten could slip into the Japanese army and slaughter many hundred before sunrise. Ghosts in the night."

Gloria watched Mr. Yun's unblinking eyes, and imagined what he saw. She enjoyed his stories of ancient times and their visits to the echoes, across the street from the Lotte Mart, up the hill in the Bongeunsa Temple.

She touched his shoulder. He blinked and the stealth cuts from tight-gripped *Jingeom* and *Ingeom* swords empowered by the spirits of dragons and tigers, leather armor emblazoned with the great Phoenix, and the whole of the Goryeo Kingdom, was lost to the code on the screen.

Yun turned to her. "Do not use your weapons just because you have them. Wait for the right battle." He wrapped his fingers around her head and gave her a playful shake. "Remember that in times of peace, the man of war will attack himself."

"Is that an old Buddhist saying?"

"No." He turned off the computer. "Nietzsche. Let's sit."

Her eyelids closed and she followed her breath. The peaceful flow of his words, the Diamond Sutra, vibrated her skin. She knew her father would not approve, and smiled.

She tried to change her last name but her father would not let her. Gloria Stiles, the daughter of Graham Stiles, the CEO of Stiles Industry, a global conglomerate of biotech firms, real estate, retail stores, e-commerce and internet gaming. She wanted anonymity; he wanted her to be proud. But of what, she thought. Her birth mother was locked up in an institution, and her father's second wife was young enough to be her big sister—a tired cliché. At every stumble, he was there with influence and cash to pick her up. She rubbed her knee, a torn meniscus from a biking accident. She refused to have it replaced: a small victory.

When the news of Mr. Yun's death reached her in America, she was a sophomore at the University of Pennsylvania. There would be no opportunity to pay her last respects. His funeral was small. His final wishes were to bypass all tradition, exclude a procession, or lengthy mourning, just a simple Buddhist burial.

There was no getting past the name. Everyone wanted to talk to the daughter of Graham Stiles. How many Lamborghinis had he crashed? Was he really good friends with the Russian president? What were going to be his next big investments?

When offered the pill at her first, and only, frat party, she considered popping it in her mouth, and washing it down with a gulp of beer. "It will help you relax," the young man said. "It's nothing big." He smiled with too many teeth.

She held the pill, examined it, saw the cross-score, thought of taking it, losing control, waking up in a strange bed that smelled of stale beer and puke. Maybe pregnant. That would teach her father for forcing her to go to this school. She wanted MIT.

"Flunitrazepam," she said. The guy shrugged. "A roofie? Very old-school." She plopped the pill in his beer. "You take it." She left.

She lost track of Mr. Yun after her father moved them back to the states. Mr. Yun was grateful for the opportunity to be responsible for another man's daughter, but weary of modern ways, the synthetic reality of computers. He renounced his old life, adopted the Buddhist way of *woonsuseung*, and became a cloud-water monk: no fixed residence, nomadic, helping others. Gloria found this romantic, and sad; she yearned for the attachment with Mr. Yun, but he'd let her go.

When the package arrived from Korea, she unrolled it, and placed it on her wall. It was beautiful. A large drawing from Mr. Yun, pencil on Hanji paper. It portrayed a large, white expanse, with a single ant in the bottom right hand corner. The insect stood: defiant, upright, and alone in the void. A singularity. It appeared to look out over the space beyond the paper. Was it a beginning, or an ending? Tears streamed down Gloria's cheeks. She felt like a visitor in her life. She shut her eyes and said a prayer to Mr. Yun. She asked for help. She knew he would hear her plea.

IN THE SILENT BASEMENT of OCSN, Gloria imagined Mr. Yun's voice. Chanting.

Gloria's job with a third tier bio-tech firm that rolled out cheap generics on expired patents did not gain Graham Stiles's approval, but he let the battle go in his daughter's favor. He felt he was winning the war.

Her teeth crunched more onions and she pressed the enter key. She reached out in a stretch and imagined butterfly wings and whispered, "Homage to the perfection of wisdom, the lovely, the holy."

TIM AND CAROL BRAITHWAITE sipped coffee at their kitchen table. They feigned calm for each other, and this made things worse. Don't think of a white elephant! Pretend *she's* not thinking of a white elephant. Smile. In their heads, a caged beast with Jackson Pollock's face paced back and forth; it sneered and threw color from paint-laden brushes to splatter and drip horrific thoughts down brain crevices; it would never make any sense, never coalesce into art. News was on the way. They waited, and hoped, and wondered about their place in what had become a mess of a world.

It had been happening everywhere, every day, all day, for over two months. The emissary teams made their deliveries and unfortunate pick-ups in bright red vans: UPS trucks with a new name and fresh paint job.

Tim remembered going through the big layoff at work two years ago: a quarter of his department was to be axed. He had to sit by his phone in his cubicle, aside everyone else, to wait for a call. If his phone rang, he would be summoned down to HR. He sat, as one by one the circuit breakers in his nervous system overloaded, light replaced by darkness, hoping for the best, expecting the worst. Listening to his heart pound for six hours before the all clear was announced over the PA system. In comparison, those were the good old days.

"Maybe we should just run," she said. "Cut the chips out of our arms and go."

"Run where?" He looked around the room. "Let's trust the system."

Tim watched Carol look at her coffee and turn her wedding ring around her finger.

"You'll wear off the inscription if you keep that up," he said. "Do you remember the word?"

"Forever," she said.

"Yes, forever." How would the knock on the door sound? Perhaps an amicable *rap, rap, rap*, from a guy with a simple germ mask and a messenger bag, or, an iron-fisted *bang, bang, bang*, from a helmeted SWAT team equipped with 5,000 volt tasers and adaptive assault rifles?

The mandatory testing rolled across the country with a fearsome efficiency. It was too competent and well-planned, a drill that had been practiced in secret at some clandestine government base, the hammer waiting for a nail conspiracy theorists preached about. Voices rose up in protest. Human rights are being violated! Democracy is yielding to dictatorship! But the boisterous chinwaggers on all media outlets got in line, or went away.

Some would rip open the envelope, others if they were not sedated, tased, or shot, let it sit for days. That one bold word on top, what would it be? ACTIVE. CARRIER. DORMANT. CLEAR.

Reality had changed six months ago when the President, in an unprecedented three-hour broadcast, outlined the plans for dealing with what he called, "the plague of our lifetime…a global crisis." He referenced the names of prestigious scientists and institutions, described the distribution of portable microRNA testing equipment, gestured in the air to illustrate the Reed-Frost Epidemic Model, intertwined his fingers to show unity and cooperation among global leaders. All anyone heard was the unequivocal result: cancer was contagious. May God bless you, and may God bless the United States of America.

Tim counted the revolutions Carol's ring made and gave in to the erosion of his atheism. He started to pray.

Then came the knock.

GLORIA STILL LIKED BOOKS, but had limited space in her apartment, and was particular about additions to her collection. The one handed to her by the used bookstore clerk did not quite fit her penchant for old medical tomes on cancer.

"Heck of a title, huh? *Colorectal Cancer: A Physician's Journey.* I put it aside just for you." The hipster clerk crumpled up the Post-it note with Gloria's name, threw it three feet toward a trashcan, and missed. "I keep my eye out for your stuff," the clerk said. "Medical…?"

"Medical Anthropology," Gloria said. The clerk's skin was a variation of burlywood, one of the newer colors trending this month. Last month he was urban chartreuse, then all the rage with glam punkers.

"Right." The clerk held up a trumpet. He'd found it trash picking. "Just a few dents but it seems OK," he said. Gloria also took advantage of the piles of property landlords had to throw out when their rich tenants graduated and moved on. A benefit of living in a top tier college town. He blew into the instrument. "That was supposed to be a b-flat, but it sounds more like a b-fart. Ha, Ha…I'm saving up for a dexterity virus. It'll take me a few months to put together the cash, blew everything I had on my new skin." He pulled out the brass mouthpiece, pointed it at a ceiling light and looked through it. "What do you think, you buying that?"

She nodded and handed over some cash. "I like it. Good eye."

"Excellento." He made change. "Don't you think they got it backwards?"

She shrugged. "Got what backwards?"

"I think viruses should be free and we should pay for school. Right? Doesn't that make more sense?"

She took the bag. "I guess."

"Sure thing." She grabbed the door and wanted to get out. In another minute the clerk would be mentioning her father's very public donation to retool the mini-particle accelerator lab. Gloria hated her notoriety, her father's public presence, even though it jumped her up the waiting list and into school.

"Right-ee-o." He gave her a thumbs up, and she noticed his palms were greenish, still in transition. "See you next week. I'll keep on the lookout out for more good stuff."

GLORIA LOOKED THROUGH her book collection. With her recent purchase, she had 46 volumes; her favorites were about cancer. She was still fascinated that this disease had taken so long to stamp out. A friend's recommendation to read Kuhn's *The Structure of Scientific Revolutions* started her journey on understanding blind spots and paradigm shifts. The idea that cancer had ever been a death sentence seemed ridiculous.

The alarm on her watch sounded and administered a slight shock to her wrist. She changed her shirt, slipped three empty blood vials into the waistband of her panties, and headed out to Greenwood Estates.

Gloria volunteered at Greenwood, which was one of several underground hospice centers that emerged with the trend in virus-free living. They were not quite legal.

She smiled at the receptionist and walked to the back room where she sat with the dying. A part of her hated these people who'd let themselves get old and sick; those who'd refused, for religious or other moral reasons, to get virus upgrades. But she liked to pick their brains about the days when diseases were not curable, when teeth had to be drilled, joints replaced, arteries shunted, organs removed, the hunt and peck of chemotherapy, and the barbaric practice of exploratory surgery.

A part of her understood, and was attracted to their thinking, seeing beauty and art in the quest for, and acceptance of, imperfection and impermanence.

The missing link is how she described this era in her dissertation: the connection that stretched back to the use of leeches, bloodletting, and other types of barbarism, perpetrated by an unenlightened society. While the medical community was trying to eradicate viruses, and tech companies worked to create weapons for biological warfare, mistakes were made, and recognized. A new class of genetically modified viruses arose from failed experiments to repair and improve cell structure and reproduction. Epidemiological mercenaries transported with a transdermal patch, and ta-da, a fixed body.

Majors in Genomics were in demand. Gloria was well on her way to completing her Ph.D. Her dissertation was done, but she did not submit it, so that she could have continued access to the labs for her passion project. The university labs were not monitored the way commercial labs were, and she could tinker without attracting any attention.

She reached two fingers into her pants and slipped out one of the vials. She sat next to Mr. Sanderson, a Seventh Day Adventist, who ran a tailor shop, and refused to have his pancreatic cancer cured. Ugly tumors mangled his organs into a rusted junkyard, an inelegant steampunk nightmare. "Hi, Mr. Sanderson," Gloria said. "How are you today?"

"Still dying." He spoke a command, and his bed raised him upright.

"Aren't we all?" It was their usual greeting. The evolutionary rate of genetic engineering knowledge and its application eclipsed every previous scientific revolution; assumptions rose and fell; new paradigms spawned innovative benefits and lucrative businesses. Bio-tech companies grew money, one cell conversion at a time.

The commercialization of body-mods blew a financial bubble of medical research that raged for twenty-five years with no burst in sight. Society had become a delirious, reimagined version of itself.

"You look pretty today," Mr. Sanderson said. "What have you done to yourself?"

"So I don't look pretty all the time? Just today?" She took a deep breath, expanded her chest, and held it in for a few seconds.

"I'm just making small talk."

"I know," Gloria said. "You just like me because I'm *au-nature*, freckles and all." These damaged folks, and their attitude of self-destruction had rubbed off on her. Gloria recognized and admired their authenticity. She used a reset virus to upset her father, and reverted to some of her birth genes: dirty blonde hair, brown eyes, white skin covered with freckles and moles.

She leaned over to let Mr. Sanderson get a peek down her shirt at her breasts. Then she touched the vial to his leg, the one mottled red and desensitized by a blood clot, and drew blood. He smiled when she pulled back with exaggerated modesty and wagged a finger at him. "Naughty, naughty, Mr. Sanderson." She slipped the full vial back down her pants. "How about I read to you?"

"Something real," he said. "Hemingway. My favorite." He looked her in the eye; a lost art; a gaze that reached across and let her know she, too, was mortal. It reassured her. He shut his eyes.

From memory, she recited the first lines of his favorite: *The Old Man and the Sea*. "He was an old man who fished alone in a skiff in the Gulf Stream, and he had gone eighty-four days now without taking a fish."

Mr. Sanderson fell asleep, sooner than usual, and she drew two more vials of his blood.

THE INTRODUCTION OF engineered viruses that attacked cells with *friendly fire* replications enabled a DNA reformation. Mimicking the viruses they created, the application of this technique gave rise to cures for almost anything. Injection treatments fixed pancreases to cure diabetes; into the eye membrane to cure macular degeneration; into joints to rec-reate healthy cartilage. Creams to eradicate wrinkles and restore skin elasticity, virus infusion for the brain to cure Alzheimer's, Parkinson's and ALS. This held such positive hope it gave rise to the thinking that man could live well beyond one hundred, two hundred, even five hundred years. The idea of immortality was debated as a blessing and a curse.

GLORIA WATCHED Mr. Sanderson's erratic breaths; he'd stop, and then gasp—the sound of a pig inhaling slop—then stop. She wondered: sleep apnea or death rattle? The b-fart from the chartreuse bookstore clerk's trumpet sounded in her head.

Gloria's dissertation changed her: *Biosocial Variation and the Intensification of Diminished Anthropomorphic Characteristics in Homo Sapiens.* Her conclusion was that with perfection, the human race was no longer human. She called it *Homo Nulla.* Her anger increased. She needed to rip flawlessness apart. Tear it down and wander through the rubble. Science was creating more than immortals. The application to brain cells balanced serotonin levels, and proved a cure for depression, ADHD, and addiction. Synaptic pathways were mapped and supercharged to create increases in intelligence; memory, abstract thought, factual organization… an ability to see the future. Muscle growth and performance was increased; anyone could choose to be a top athlete, a virtuoso on any instrument in the orchestra, a master representational oil painter.

The effect on society was dramatic. At first there were the haves and the have-nots. But business leaders primed government pumps, and worked out a distribution rate to create a balance to hold their advantage.

Prejudices were eliminated. Skin tone became a fashion statement; each year new color became the fad: blues, greens, and rainbow, perhaps even the retro hues of black and white. Sexual orientation was a choice and could be altered on demand: heterosexuality declined; bringing new lives into the world was discouraged.

Everyone was an artist. Everyone was a scholar. Old structures and industries collapsed. Schools were no longer required. Competitive sports were boring to watch. The high-paying elites were those focused on building and maintaining infrastructure: plumbers, electricians, and carpenters.

Politicians were subjected to genetic alteration and rendered unable to lie.

Military applications shaped a new world peace.

Religious difference was the only outstanding conflict, as it had been for eternity, and in light of scientific advances, with so little unknown about human nature and morality, their hold was fading. The creator was man; God was on his way out.

Disease and imperfection was outlawed. Consumerism was the only weapon in the battle against boredom.

The search for meaning became fruitless. Suicide clubs emerged.

Gloria's dissertation had become a treatise for a revolution. She wanted to be a rebel, reject it all. She sat with the dying, hoping for answers in the shadows. She collected her samples, flawed building blocks, pure in their defects.

A door was presented to her. A discovery. One loose thread that needed a pull; it was uncovered as it started, by noticing a mistake.

THE BRAITHWAITES LOOKED UP in unison as the ET truck rumbled up their driveway. When only a deliveryman stepped onto their porch they breathed a sigh of relief. It meant that neither of them would be ushered off to a detention center. At least for now. Tim and Carol, as dictated by law, signed for their envelopes with a fingerprint read and a retinal scan. No words passed between them and the courier, and his eyes showed no emotion over the filtration mask that covered his face.

They let the bright red envelopes sit on their kitchen table for several minutes before opening them. Although they considered themselves agnostics, their minds wandered to the possibility of a god; if he, she, or it, did exist, they silently prayed for good news, as though the words on the paper in the envelopes might change.

Carol picked up both envelopes and felt their weight, thickness, looking for an indication of the news they might hold. She handed Tim his envelope and he held it in both hands, rotating it back and forth. They seized on the present they both now shared: to exist for a few more moments before they discovered the reality of their future.

She asked again. "Can we run away? I don't want to be apart from you."

"We'll be fine," he sighed. "They'll find a cure. How can they not?"

As though rehearsed, in unison, they popped the seals, opened the silent messengers, pulled out the contents. Each contained five pages of data and instructions, with their status on big, bold letters on top of the first page. Their hearts pounded as they read the news, once, then again. Tim looked up as Carol sat her paper flat on the table. They looked into each other's eyes. They knew each other too well, and felt a gulf open up, a vast distance, Tim reached out and held her hand, never loving her more, and feeling alone.

IT WAS THREE IN THE MORNING. Gloria was at her day job interning at the OCSN genetic labs. Which is where she found the mistake that unfolded the discovery that would let her change mankind. It would eventually give rise to the President's speech, the internment camps, the emissary teams kicking in doors, and her role as a revolutionary leader.

The incompatible scientific framework that was uncovered seemed so impossible and implausible that it was disregarded by the other medical technicians and senior scientists as a simple error in process, or a rookie error in data analysis. But Gloria and her infinite curiosity and mild boredom had a hunch, and she dug deeper.

Two rats died. Both were in the same cage and mature. This was no big deal, lab rats died every day and, unless they were being used in a testing phase, they were just incinerated. Gloria decided to run a DNA code sequence, practicing running the software she was recently trained to use.

The satisfying crunch as she bit into her cold grilled cheese sandwich was comforting; she hated when they got soggy. Over the weeks it became easier to ignore the rules about food in the lab. A single high-powered lamp off to the side lighted her desk. The other twenty desks were empty, quiet. Through a large glass pane, LCDs blinked red, white, and green in cadence with the data being crunched through the large quantum computer. She volunteered to take on third shift full-time rather than rotate, which was well-received by the other interns.

At the biweekly intern meetings, everyone complained about their bosses, overly conservative lab rules, bullshit paperwork, senior scientists looking over their shoulders, chastising them on excessive CPU usage. Looking, nodding, shaking her head at the appropriate moments, an unconscious pantomime of body language that gave the impression of engagement as she thought about experimenting with different cheeses for her lunch, deciding to perhaps give Jarlsberg a go.

Access to the BlueGene quantum computer was highly restricted during the day, allowing only top priority analysis to take up the precious CPU time. The batch programs running at night never taxed the system's full capability, so Gloria could write and run experimental analysis without risking the wrath of management. She planned on going on for a second Ph.D., focusing on zoology, wanting to twiddle with intragenic processes, get into the pet business, applying the art and science of her vocation to create some new species. A cat with iridescent, blue-green fur, perhaps glow in the dark, no one had done that yet. Almost everything else had been brought to life.

If she did live to be five hundred, she thought of focusing on painting or music at some point, for fifty years perhaps, then maybe go for the big bucks as a plumber.

She ran the program twice, checked her inputs: the traceability of the rats' blood samples, conversion factors, and equation constants. She ran and reran equipment calibrations, traced the standards used in the calibrations. Same results.

Moving to her front row seat at the genetic revolution circus had initially been exciting: bumbling E. coli clowns, dancing protein aggregates, viral cars crammed with endlessly streaming mitochondria midgets, the jaw dropping magic of DNA biobricks, she triggered chromosomes that bounded through quantum hoops of quark-fire.

Going backstage was a bit horrifying: results were always clearly known about these processes but the exact action mechanisms were still a theory. Mathematical bio-models could predict with 98% certainty the effects of these discoveries, but that 2%, getting comfortable with the uncertainty and not knowing what was not known, took some time getting used to.

No one questioned the science anymore. Like the theory of evolution, the theory of the start of the universe, the theory of genetic modifications was taken as fact. The scientific community was sure about genetics, but so was the world when rudimentary telescopes led them to believe there were canals on Mars; before a better view showed them to be natural canyons. As the scientific viewpoint changed, movies about Martian invasions gave way to stories of colonizing the lifeless planet. Perhaps there were ancient civilizations, the ones who made the giant face on the planet, until that too was found to be just a naturally formed mountain. Genetic theory would also topple; Gloria would pull the curtain back on the new horizon, a beginner's mind seeing what was clouded to the vision of experts.

Cheese strung out from her mouth in a long ribbon, refusing to break, and she ran the analysis again. It was conclusive. One rat caught the cancer from the other. Trojan DNA that stayed dormant until just the right moment, had come to life, bonded with carbon dioxide and passed from the lungs of one rat to the other. An impossibility, until she proved it to be true.

She was fired for misuse of company property; her results deemed heretical, precious CPU time wasted. She was escorted from the premises, hiding data and the codes for the backdoors she installed in the BlueGene system in a place that would make her mommy blush.

Quality control at the labs was poor. Old code was never reviewed. When operating systems had been upgraded, automatic changes to other parts of the system was routine. She embedded code commands to initiate the replication of the Trojan DNA in every manufacturing formula. It was subtle, untraceable, and on its way.

Two months later she watched the president of the U.S. speaking on TV. Sitting on her couch, never hearing her name, she ate a grilled cheese sandwich, camembert and gouda, a good combination. Three months later she received her own test results and was rated CLEAR.

Stiles brushed away the crumbs that had dropped from her mouth to her keyboard. She put down the grilled parmesan and brie, which she thought was just OK, and logged onto BlueGene.

TIM WAS CLEAR, his genetic makeup had a tight bio structure that made him immune to all the mutations of the Trojan virus and its contagious protein structures that cut into healthy DNA to replicate.

Carol was DORMANT, which is why she had some time before she was taken away. Her dormancy showed Level 5 propensities for breast cancer: a 90% certainty. Since the exact time of a Trojan virus attack on the body was unknown, she was sent to one of local isolation centers, where she would be monitored with a daily blood test, allowed to do work shuffling around data, and spend thirty minutes a week on a monitored video call with Tim.

The containment camps sprung up in a matter of weeks. The efficiency of their rise left no doubt that the government had them well planned in advance, on the books waiting for the right threat: prefab buildings, wired and secured, military personnel pre-aligned to duties never seen during peacetime.

Of the approximately 400 million U.S. residents, 250 million were labeled ACTIVE, having cancer cells that were overtaking their bodies; new tests, too expensive for routine checking before the plague, picked up tiny traces of aberrant cells even if they had not yet disrupted any other body functions. Fifty million were CARRIERS, Trojan viruses coursing through their systems, previously undetected, waiting for yet undetermined conditions to replicate. The twenty-five million DORMANT patients had weaknesses in their genetic structure, with favorable conditions for a Trojan virus but non-detected. The remainders were CLEAR, no viruses, Trojan or otherwise, and tight genetic structures making them immune.

TIM SAT IN A PARK and looked out at the city buildings. The Internet was shut down, security over satellite networks was tight, television was limited to one channel endlessly scrolling through information reports, warnings, every other night a one-hour live broadcast giving an update on the situation. Absent was discussion of life after a solution, after science solved this as they had every other problem. Everyone was now a government employee, food and water was plentiful, picked up on a daily basis from the sterilization locations that had sprung up with the containment centers. Payment was evidence of up to date monthly blood tests.

"Papers," requested a security officer. Tim allowed the uniformed official to swipe a reader over his forearm where his data chip was installed. A beep and, "Thank you, sir." Tim watched him walk away, tearing down a flyer off of a telephone pole, neatly folding it and putting it in his pocket. It was the same one Tim had hidden in his pocket.

The multitude of sharp-angled buildings of the city stretched up, mirrored windows reflected the rising sunlight, and captured images of passing clouds. The buildings sat empty, closed. Tim and Carol were architects, now considered non-essential functions, leaving him to wait, for what he was not sure.

A handful of other strangers sat on benches and stared into nothing, never making contact with anyone else but the occasional uniformed agent, himself alone, passing the time between scans. A couple, fortunate to have each other, sat further down the walkway. They held hands, motionless. Lucky for them to have each other, thought Tim, not knowing, and not choosing to speculate, on the silent horrors they shared, children that may have been taken away, the fear of bad results on their next test. Carol spoke to him of other couples with the same rating, a curse that blessed those able to live together inside the internment camps. His CLEAR rating was a spiritual death sentence: loneliness, boredom, endless hours waiting for something to change.

The cool air passed through his nostrils and into his lungs. He no longer took the auto response of breathing for granted. He noticed each breath, followed it, became seated in the moment.

Tim's mind raced through scenarios, opportunities where he might be reunited with Carol. Many who did not have a significant other to keep them going chose to exit life, suicide, a growing epidemic, not something the government cared to control. There were rumors, brief words spoken at the food centers about clandestine activist groups, planning to do something, to take back control.

When the official moved out of sight, Tim took out the flyer, an announcement of a meeting, no details on where, or when, or with whom, just a meeting, a small stencil of Che Guevara on the bottom right-hand corner.

He folded the piece of paper and stuffed it back in his pocket. It was hope for some action. He was not sure what. Deliverance? His wish was simple, to be reunited with Carol, he would do anything.

"Care for a water?" The man sat down on the bench next to him. Close-cropped beard, average height, retro-white skin, a light blue short sleeve shirt showing the chip spot on his arm, smartly dressed, perhaps an ex-broker when there was still a Wall Street trading stocks. "It's an extra, seal's not broken. It's clean."

"No thanks." Tim turned back to the cloud reflections.

"Loved one, perhaps?"

"What?"

"I saw you took one of those flyers. That's how we are doing this you know." He spoke with a calm assurance, getting right to the point. "Strange, a flyer with no information. We watch. We watch for anyone who takes one, and then we make contact."

Tim turned. "How do you make contact?"

"Like this. We watch, and see who lingers over the posts that say nothing. Who might rip down this nothing and take it. Like you." He again offered the water bottle. Tim took it. "We can try and get you what you need."

"How do you know what I need?" Tim twisted the bottle open, and took a small sip; then a bigger sip. He drank half the bottle. He turned to the man. "I'm sorry, I didn't realize I was so thirsty."

"It's OK," the man said. "Want to meet some people? We can go now." The man stood up, confident that Tim would follow. "Let's walk. It's not far."

Tim stood and followed.

A few blocks away, on a tree-lined side street, sat a brick, four-story apartment building. Two guys sat on the stoop, rippling biceps, both some shade of green-brown. With a brief exchange of nods, they lumbered to their feet; both men took a look around the street as Tim and his new acquaintance entered.

Tim was instructed to sit on the couch as the man disappeared into another room.

Just an apartment Tim thought. He heard a cat meowing in another room. What would they ask? How would he answer? Was he ready to join an armed group, ready to storm a detention center, ready to risk his life to rescue Carol? He wished they had run away.

In the corner, a TV played the government channel, books were stacked here and there, the furniture looked second hand. Were there stores of weapons in the back? Would they emerge with a loaded rifle, grenades, and flak jackets?

Tim stood when the man returned with a young woman. "We can reunite you with your wife," she said.

Tim wondered how long they'd had their eyes on him. He started to say something but just sighed.

"I should explain," the young woman said. "We've never met before right?" She turned to the man, who nodded; an act they've performed before. "We scanned your arm chip when you entered, simple technology, cross-referenced you in the database and see that your wife Carol is interned. Bad news though, tonight, you are going to find out she is now ACTIVE. Breast cancer. Just starting. She will still have a long life, but she will be moved across state. We don't have much time, so you need to decide right now if you want to be with her."

"Of course I do!" He imagined the plan: intercept her transport truck, a team dressed in green fatigues with lots of pockets for extra ammo, grenades; there would be gunfire, explosions, and they would hug briefly before speeding off in a getaway car, to somewhere, together.

"Do you know a virus replicates 500,000 copies of itself in just twenty-four hours?" she said.

"No." He imagined he and Carol in the Pacific Northwest, in the woods, living off the land, making love under a full moon.

"Your next blood test is just two days away so we have to do this now." She held out a syringe.

"I don't understand?" Tim said.

"I retrieved your genomic profile," the woman said, "quickly modified a virus, added a few protein dips, RNA twists, and it's ready to go."

"I'm not following you," Tim said. "I'm CLEAR. How do we rescue Carol?"

"We can't get her out, but we can get you in." She gave him a few seconds. "Not what you expected, huh? It's the best we can do. I can give you the same type of genetic illness as Carol. In two days you'll be whisked away to an internment camp. Reunited." She held up the needle. "It's not for certain, but I'm 99% sure I got it."

"They'll find a cure," Tim said. "They have to."

She shook her head. "There is no cure. Not anymore." She shook the needle. "If you walk away now, there won't be a second chance."

Tim felt rushed. He wanted to go away . . . think about it . . . wait for something to feel right.

"Do you believe in God?" the woman said. "Heaven and Hell?"

"I'm trying," Tim said.

She shook the needle. "It's right here."

"Which is it?" Tim said. "Heaven, or Hell?"

She shrugged.

Tim extended his arm, looked away, felt the needle prick his skin and a warm dab from what he guessed was an alcohol-soaked cottonball. "Hold this and keep your arm bent for a few minutes. You might get nauseous. Then we'll know it worked. But it will pass quickly."

"What happens to me when they find you?"

"We're careful," She said. "We move. Clouds on water. I'll get you a sandwich, I've been messing with Blue Castello and Compte, it will be the best, believe me." She turned and looked back. "Do you like raw onions?" Then she laughed. "Probably not, who does?" Tim noticed her limp. She kissed her hand and touched it to a framed drawing, before leaving the room.

He looked at the drawing, a single ant alone on a vast landscape.

Tim heard a meow and looked down to see a blue-green, luminescent cat rubbing on his legs. He reached down and it ran under a coffee table. He heard something sizzle in the other room. A delicious smell filled his nostrils, his stomach grumbled and he tried to remember when he'd last eaten. The cat peeked out from under the table; he reached to touch its color, but it pulled back under. He saw another oddity and grabbed a newspaper from the table. He scanned the headlines. *Billionaire Graham Stiles dead. Prostate cancer ravaging college campuses.*

Tim prayed for the health of the little bug making its way through his bloodstream. He pledged and bargained to a maker he hoped was there. *Please grant me this one wish.* He pleaded to be a lucky one. He hoped he and Carol could be together. Forever.

He invoked the holy name of every God he'd ever heard about. He hoped beyond hope he would get cancer.

Already Seen

"But that's your name," the man said.

"It isn't," the kid said. "How could you know?" They sat in a small room: an off-white, utilitarian, rectangular box; way too clean, framed with indifferent right angles; a metallic smell from nothing in particular hanging in the room's chilly air. The man and the kid sat on either side of a table that was bolted to the floor. There was a wall-sized mirror behind the man. Also one door—locked.

"I have it here on all these documents," the man said. "Your psych analysis, the police report…" The man flipped his thumb along the edges of the pages making the sound of an unlucky hand of cards being shuffled; shoved them back into a coffee-stained, or was it bloodstained, manila folder, and slid the folder to the side.

The kid saw something swirl behind the mirror, a gray murmuration amid glints of tin. "Have you ever seen northern lights?" the kid said without looking at the man.

"I ask the questions here," the man said.

The kid looked at the man. "Have you ever seen northern lights?"

"No, have you?"

"Yes," the kid said. "Seeing them changed my life."

"Where did you see them?"

"On a computer."

"That's not seeing them," the man said.

"Why not?"

"It's not real," the man said.

"What you're calling me is not real," the kid said. "Not my name."

"Well, what is your name?"

"My name cannot be pronounced, or known," the kid said. "Unaware, infinite, void, and complete. Ein Sof."

"Have you ever taken LSD, psychedelic mushrooms…?"

"No."

"You sure?"

"I'd know." The kid looked over the man's shoulder. "I know everything."

The man laid his hand, palm down, on the manila folder. "Why did you do it?"

"I had no choice."

"Everyone has a choice." The man glanced at the folder as though it might offer proof of all the rotten choices to be had.

"No one has any choices." The kid looked past the man. "Who's behind the glass?"

"It's just a mirror."

"Two way?"

"Maybe."

"Well, we're there," the kid said, pointing.

The man turned around, then turned back. "What do you mean?"

"Our faces. Our bodies."

"Just a reflection."

"You sure?" the kid said.

"You're pleading not guilty?" the man said.

"Correct."

"But you said you did it."

"Correct."

"Why were you hiding in the bottom of the closet in your apartment?"

"I hide because I'm tired of seeing."

"Seeing what?"

"Everything. The past. The future." The kid looked into the mirror. "Me—a ghost moving through it all. Stuck in it all. The present. The now. It's tiring. I'm tired of looking at it."

"There's a medical term for this." The man said. "Temporal lobe epilepsy: permanent *déjà vu*. You've been here before. You will always forever be here before. It's like a lesson in English. Verb tenses. What difference do they make? You're always just where you are. I feel for you kid, really. That's what I'm saying." In the mirror the kid watched the man touch his head. "A wiring problem in the brain." The man snapped erect and pointed at the kid. "Don't do that."

"Do what?" the kid said. "I'm just sitting here."

"Well," the man said, "don't do what you were going to do."

"What was I going to do? How do you know?"

"I know. You don't. No one said life was fair."

In the mirror, the kid watched his hand touch his head, mimicking the man's previous gesture. "Must be contagious." The man paused and squinted. "What's wrong?" the kid said.

"Just a funny feeling," the man said. "Something familiar."

"*Very* contagious," the kid said.

The kid saw in the mirror a reflection of the picture his grandmother had on her fireplace mantle: he was twelve years old, dressed in a blue Catholic grade school blazer, the crooked smile on his face showed displeasure, no, the kid remembered, it was pain.

The kid stood up, raised both his hands, made fists, and brought them down in unison, his knuckles *thwacked* three times on the table. He walked to the open door, and as he passed through, he took a peripheral glance at his face in the mirror: very old, almost dead.

The door slammed shut behind him. Locked.

"He's not insane," the kid said to the four people sitting at the observation table.

"How can you tell?" the police officer said. "You were in there about two minutes and didn't speak a word." The officer checked that the door was locked. He glanced at his watch.

The kid peered through the one-way glass at the back of the man's head. "I just know." The kid searched for his own reflection, but it was gone.

"You'll sign off on this?" the officer said.

"Yes," the kid said.

"You're the expert," the officer said. "As long as you sign off on the paperwork, I don't give a shit. He's not insane. Fine. That means he's sane, right?"

"Right," the kid said.

A woman at the table wearing a light charcoal-colored pants suit stood up. "We just got sandwiches," she said. "Didn't get a chance to eat yet." She pointed at a round, plastic, silver-colored tray. "Do you want one?"

The kid looked at the sandwiches. He thought they were turkey or chicken, surely some kind of bird.

The Descent

Paul Sharp was on his hands and knees trying to drink out of the toilet but gave up. He wondered how dogs did this and guessed it had to do with their long tongues. So he grabbed the cup off the sink and dipped it in. He knew the cup was clean, an ornament in the first-floor guest bathroom, never used, unlike the one in the master bedroom that was always full of toothbrushes and disposable razors. He emptied the cup with one gulp and filled it again. He took sips and tried to decipher the taste: gin, scotch, vodka, and a hint of bourbon? It went down smoothly and warmed his belly. He was good for now but stopped short of pushing the silver lever for a flush.

He decided it was a good day for a small adventure. He felt like exploring, and the persistent heat and lack of rain created the proper conditions. The county had issued its first-ever water usage restrictions. The grass on the manicured portion of his small farmette was brown and cracked underfoot; the vegetable gardens bore only remnants of life with evenly spaced tomato cages and beanpoles, cluttered with withered vines. The shallow spring pond, normally thriving with tadpoles, was dried up. He guessed that the old well at the back of the property would be empty and ready for a descent.

He was drinking coffee and listening to the news on NPR. The U.S. Department of Homeland Security had issued a warning based on credible chatter about suicide bombers with small nukes; an unusually powerful solar flare was streaming towards the earth which might knock out electronics; NASA's deep space telescopes had identified a new type of black hole dubbed Planet Killer; and the stock market opened down.

His wife was visiting her sister in Colorado for a long weekend, and he was starting a month long break, back from Hong Kong where he trained pilots on flight simulators. It was one of the perks of his job, free plane tickets, and he was happy manning the fort while she helped her sister, recently divorced, get set up in a new place. He wished they had parted on better terms, but her plans for a romantic evening after his two-month absence were ruined by his drinking. They had a big fight and she made him promise to abstain while she was gone. He swore an oath and showed his resolve by emptying the liquor cabinet into the toilet.

Sharp stepped onto the back deck. He took in the large oak and black walnut trees surrounding his home and, in the distance, the property's enormous red barn. A low rumble above caused him to look up, he watched a distant plane, its contrails sharp white lines that expanded their signature as the jet moved across the sky. He wanted to be back up there, above the ground, empowered by the freedom of flight, moving with purpose, defying gravity, far removed from the trivial activity of the insect life below. It was the only place he felt whole.

His time in the air had started with a four-year tour flying C-130 cargo planes in Vietnam. He had a fifteen-year stint as a construction worker, then enlisted in the reserves to get recertified as a pilot before the cutoff age of forty. In Desert Storm he spent his nights circling above the Middle East, again in a C-130, its large cargo bay retrofitted as a communication center, packed with electronic equipment monitoring ground transmissions, and occasionally issuing fake commands and coordinates to the Iraqi ground forces that caused them to send shell fire onto each other. He passed his days in the desert, reading briefs, working out, waiting to lift off from the runway. After the military he flew commercial jets until the age of sixty-five, when he was forced into retirement with a lost pension from a bankrupt airline.

The simulator pay was good and he enjoyed creating disasters, watching students panic: one engine failing, two engines failing, total loss of hydraulics with piercing alarms, flashing panel lights, the cabin a mechanical bull ride throwing them into complete disorientation. He taught the trainees to remain calm, assess the situation, turn off their emotions and determine the best next step. Between lessons, he'd often sit alone in the cockpit, bored with fighting induced calamities, cruising the imaginary skies of the world, disconnected in the darkness.

His roof had a leak that needed repair but, with the lack of rain, it could wait. Wearing a camping light on his head and carrying a garden trowel, he followed the path behind the pond through brambles and fallen branches, until he reached the downtrodden and rusted barbed wire that circled the well.

He knew the well was about a hundred years old and long abandoned. When they bought the place, the realtor suggested it was a safety hazard, an imperfection on the property that should be filled in.

He visited the well many times, and he imagined the farmer that built it, digging down who knows how many feet, meticulously positioning the stones that fortified the walls, a life support system providing water for the family and animals that once lived on the farm. He had probed its depth with tree branches, poking down five or ten feet below the water's surface, but never hitting the bottom. He thought it might hold treasures: a tool, perhaps a pocket watch that had fallen from a farmer's pocket as he leaned over inspecting its integrity, or perhaps to extract water in a makeshift bucket lowered by hand with a sturdy line.

He turned on the headlamp and looked down. The circular caverns, built with irregular stones, made him think about the stalwart walls of European castles, set to survive their maker's impermanent flesh. It appeared bone dry, but he could not make out the bottom.

The LED beam bounced back and forth with his head movements, and he confirmed that the spaces between the stones would give him enough hand and footholds for a somewhat safe descent. As a precaution, he tied a rope around a tree, circled the other end around his waist, and secured it with a cinch knot connected to a series of carabineers hooked to his belt, a crude pulley system for lowering himself. He gave the line a few solid tugs; satisfied it would hold his weight, he started down.

When his head was below ground level, he paused to center himself, letting his eyes adjust to the nascent darkness. He could still not see the bottom. Dropping a few more feet he felt the air become cool, he heard sound muted, and felt the sunlight in further retreat. A small wrench of fear twisted in his chest before he tamped it out. Descending, he braced his back on one side, hooked his feet into the rocks on the other, and turned off his headlamp. He remembered the sun setting over the Mekong Delta, the sturdy hum of his C-130, his co-pilot asleep, radio silence, and his entrancement by the peace that insulated him from the horror on the ground. The irregular stream of MEDEVAC helicopters, the urgent shuttle of stretchers moving soldiers with gut shots, missing limbs, head wounds, all comrades, and some friends, kept at a safe distance, thirty thousand feet below. He never told Helen of these things. Could never tell her. They stayed in his head, obnoxious guests at a private party who would not leave unless he agreed to join them for one last round. He always gave in, but found them to be liars.

He turned his headlamp back on and picked up the pace, he wanted to get down, and also wanted to get back out. He dropped free-fall the last few feet, hitting bottom. He kicked at the debris covering the ground: branches, leaves, loose stones. He guessed the well was thirty feet deep. He was surprised that it was so narrow. He perceived the diameter wider during his initial descent, but now at the base, his broad shoulders rubbed against the wall with any move. He made a few adjustments to the line, adding slack, but coiled the excess rope around his hands and tested it with a few sharp tugs, before letting go.

He got his right knee down, slid his leg back until his foot touched the wall, supported his weight by pushing both his hands against the wall just above his shoulders, easing his other knee onto the floor. He had just enough room to settle on his hands and knees, the light pointing down while the top of his head touched the stone. He brushed away the leaves and sticks to one side, removed the hand shovel from his belt, and started to dig. He took a few shallow scoops, elbows scraping on the jagged stones surrounding him, searching through the silt for treasure. This went on for ten minutes before his first and only find, a pair of gold, wire-rimmed glasses. He examined them, and seeing they were still intact, he wiped them with his shirt: half frame reading glasses. He imagined the farmer using them. Glancing over the local paper before turning in. Helping his children with long division. Reading aloud a Bible chapter at a candlelit dinner table. Simpler times. Happy times. He carefully folded and slid them into his shirt pocket.

He stopped, thought he heard something up top, a sound he could not identify. Then came a concussive blast: *Whoomp!* The image of a clown in a cannon barrel flashed through his mind, he thought someone punched him in the back of his neck, his head hit the wall and he saw darkness as the headlamp shattered.

This was the third time he had been knocked out. The first was in high school, when he was checked into the boards playing hockey. He woke up on a stretcher, with the reassuring faces of his father, coach, and teammates telling him that he was going to be all right, and that they had won the game. The second time was an impromptu boxing match in the Saudi desert, something they did to pass time, place a few bets. An uppercut had dropped him and he woke to a bucket of cold water, his buddies laughed as they pulled him to his feet. Now, coming to, he was alone, at the bottom of the well.

He feared he'd had a stroke. He moved his arms and legs, twisted his back, clenched his fists, made facial gestures, smiling and frowning, everything worked. Feeling the shattered headlamp, he looked up and saw the small circle of daylight. The safety rope was draped over him, severed from the tree. His training kicked in, pushing away fear, assessing options. Just one—climb.

He unhooked the line and started to work his way up by putting his fingers and shoe tips into the cracks, but this did not work, never able to get more than a few feet before a hand or foot slipped out. He changed his strategy and braced his back against the wall, finding finger holds with his hands, his feet flat and pushing for support. He could inch up; it was a slow process, each time he rested he thought of the toilet, glad he didn't flush it.

Now out of the well, he stood and surveyed the landscape: no trees, no house, no barn, nothing for as far as he could see but smooth black earth. He touched it, the characteristics of volcanic obsidian; it was flawless, polished, and desolate. Off to the East was a valley where he knew Lake Winnebago should be, but it was not, the same smooth blackness stretched out, dipping down, and rising on the other side.

A cloudless, blue sky shrouded everything. Looking down, the ground absorbed the bright sunlight, but looking out, at certain angles, he could see a pleasant iridescence flickering over the glassine terrain. He noticed the freshness of the air, or rather the absence of anything burning. He wondered how long he had been out. He wondered what the hell had happened.

He knew there was nothing to do but walk. Walk to find out how far this emptiness extended. The county? The state? To Colorado? Perhaps the whole planet?

He stared at the well, his little ark of salvation, sheltering him from disaster. On his knees he peered over its edge, leaning in to try and see the bottom one last time.

Although he shot out his hand and snatched, he only caught air, the glasses tumbled back down. The family gone.

He stood alone, and savored the peace. But then, they banged on the door; his guests rushed in and knocked him to his knees.

And now he knew, this time, they would never leave.

Foreclosure

Jacob Beiler sat in the passenger seat of my '72 Impala.
The car idled in the middle of the cornfield. He took a
long tug on a fifth of Kessler. "It's bullshit," he said through
a whisky-burn cough.

My job was to play the mind reader: try to guess what he
was talking about. Jacob got like that when he was drunk.
He'd have these long conversations in his head and assume
since someone was sitting next to him, they heard every word.

I gave in. "What's bullshit?"

"Compact cars have no place in a derby," he said. "It's a
fucking gimmick—like wrestling midgets." He reached into
his pocket, popped something into his mouth, and washed
it down with another swig. "My family didn't risk life and
limb on the *Charming Polly* for this bullshit." His ancestors'
trip from Rotterdam to Pennsylvania in the late 1700s was
his go-to reason for disavowing all things that pissed him
off: the liberals, the Jews, the press, mega-farms, taxes, the
speed limit, a dinner date that didn't put out.

On Saturday nights at the Edgewood Fairgrounds, Jacob
and I roared around the demolition derby track in our beaters.

The feel of smashing your car into another, on purpose, with purpose, all legal, was a great release after a week of farming. Jacob drove a matte black Ford LTD, an ex-cop car. I had my parents' old Impala. Both were V8s, windows taken out, bumpers trimmed, hoods removed, and fitted with marine gas tanks. Jacob was halfway through a four-week suspension for making an illegal direct driver door hit on another racer. I didn't like how he looked at me, Jacob would explain.

There was talk that the track was going to shut down. The fan base was waning. The Epstein twins, financial advisors, inherited the business from their grandfather and tried to boost sales with the Mini-Cooper demolition races. The boys were keeping Edgewood open out of respect; when the old man died, we figured the track would close.

"We're not Dutch, you know," Jacob said. "We're German: not my fault assholes couldn't pronounce *Deutsch*."

I let that one go.

Jacob was a good friend. We had a lot in common. Oldest sons of farmers; taught to hook up teat cups; drive tractors and bailers, just after learning to walk. By the time we were twelve, we could fix anything with bailing wire, a screwdriver, and a hammer. It was understood from our fathers, that when we were of age, we would drop out of high school to farm full-time.

I married Lina, the girl next door. Neither of us had siblings, not who were alive. After our parents died, our combined farm was nine-hundred acres and three-hundred cows. Jacob's wife was a college girl. He busted his ass putting her through UW-Madison. A few weeks after she earned her MBA, she left Jacob for a product development hotshot at a California startup. She met him at Techsylvania: a global business conference in Romania. Must have been love at first bite, Jacob would say.

Jacob was never the same. He began to hate anyone in a stable relationship. A sadistic jealousy took him over. After a few drinks he would threaten to break up other marriages. He would talk of fucking other guys' wives, just to teach them a lesson.

It was after midnight. I decided to turn off the engine. A light summer breeze blew through the stalks of corn. It sounded like the crackle of a far-off fire.

"I can't believe everybody dies after a *courageous* fight with cancer!" Jacob said. "Aren't some people afraid, downright cowards even? And why do they have to say people died suddenly, or unexpectedly?" Jacob raised his voice. "Just fucking say drug overdose or suicide, for Christ's sake."

He was halfway through the bottle; it gave me a sense of relief. The more loaded he was, the easier it would be for me to go through with my plan.

We married the wrong women, he would tell me. He thought I would have been better suited for his wife, and he for my Lina. You read a lot, he would say. You worry about things, wonder how stuff works, the big stuff like governments, and banking, and foreign countries. My wife would love to talk about all that. Me, I just want to farm and fuck, drive the derby on Saturday nights.

We sat in the middle of my cornfield, in my derby vehicle, and waited for a sign of the kids who thought doing doughnuts through my rows was great summer fun. Jacob was as anxious as me to surprise them, ram into their big truck, probably their daddy's truck, and teach them a lesson. When I told Jacob, he was gung-ho to join me, more excited than I was to catch them in the act. But it would never happen: I made the story up to get Jacob out here alone.

Neither of us had any real friends, just lots of acquaintances. Farmer friends. We'd all stop for a coffee at Sassy Sals between six and seven after the cows were set. The wall was full of coffee mugs with our names on them; we drank a quick cup while we stood and complained about the weather, our faulty equipment, the banks, and our overdue loans, before getting back to it. At night we'd go across the street, between six and seven in the evening, to the Dairyland Pub, where we would ask for our engraved glass mugs and have a quick one before going home for dinner.

There were about twenty of us who would mingle. Muddy boots, the smell of cow and pig shit; we accepted all that from each other and this made us friends. Ask me anything about the guys that didn't have to do with farm complaining, and I swear I couldn't tell you a single thing. I didn't know who had a wife, kids, grandkids; maybe we'd hear about some relative dying now and then, but we paid no attention unless they were crushed in a tractor overturn, or sucked through a combine, cut up and spat out: the equipment moved fast, without a conscience, whether it gave life or took it away, it was all the same: just one stray thought while you worked, and your arm gets ripped off. The machines don't care what you wished you'd done three years ago, or the fearful stuff from your night terrors that pushed out to take a daylight peek from behind some closed door in your brain.

After enough years around this equipment, and we all turned into machines: we do what we have to, to keep moving, and we don't care who we chew up and spit out. This is the only explanation I can give for what I was going to do to Jacob.

"Racing rules are simple," Jacob spat the words. It doesn't matter how damaged you are; if you're the last one moving, you win." Another draw on the Kessler; it was almost empty. "Why isn't life like that?" He looked at me and finally offered me the bottle. I waved it off. Jacob shrugged and put it back to his lips. "I have days, plenty of days, where I just want to stop moving. Who would give a shit?" Was I supposed to say something to Jacob? Maybe, but he was right: no one would.

We all let our landlines go to save money. None of us used the social media stuff on our cell phones. Calls and texts were all. A look at messages or texts now and then was enough to put off the field madness that might set in when your head gets locked into a loop about some shit in your life. We even lost that for the better part of two weeks when Tommy Angelo got liquored up and drove his pick-up into the cell tower. He knocked the thing offline. Funny though, we all thought it was a lucky shot, but Brad Williams, the local sheriff, told me in confidence that Tommy rammed the tower over twenty times. They had him upstate in a psychiatric hospital to try and figure out what came loose in his head.

I knew what was wrong with Tommy. We all knew. The pressure, the darkness, that damned pit you fell into now and then; how hard you had to focus on the job to climb out; the deep fear that you might not make it back up to the light.

The work offered us routine, and in that, there was a solace. Endless repetition of the same tasks, day after day, year after year, the fields, the free-stall barns: our Buddhist monastery. The population of us god-ordained land monks dwindled. Equipment failure, flooding, disease, unable to keep good help, the low price of produce, the rise in loan interest…the day when putting a bullet in the head of a sick cow gave a measure of pleasure, and a six-pack and target practice with barn cats was better than sex to relieve stress.

Fifty yards ahead, I had a hole dug. I first got the idea when I thought Lina was cheating on me. Over a year, a whole year, I milked, planted seeds, fertilized, irrigated, harvested, and was absent from my own life. I planned. I even felt bad when Jacob told me that he drew up a will and made Lina and me the sole recipients of his life insurance and assets. It was an added benefit; made me wonder if he knew what I was thinking.

I got it all wrong though. The thing with Jacob and Lina was made up in my head: field madness at its worst. The hate I had for Jacob when I thought he was disrespecting me, dismantling my marriage, was so real, even after I knew it was not true, the hate still stuck to something in my core; as real as if it were true. With Lina and I about to lose the farm to the banks, I fixated on Jacob's will.

"I hate chickens," Jacob said. The bottle was empty. He started to toss it out the car window, thought twice, and put it between his legs. "Did I ever tell you about my first set of broilers? Meat birds? My fucking father?"

"No," I said.

Jacob stared straight ahead and talked. "We bought twenty-five chicks, cute little things at first. My job was to feed and water them. I just turned twelve. They grow fast. At eight weeks they were at four pounds: ready to process." He lifted the bottle, tipped it to his lips, and caught a few drops. "My dad said it was my job to kill them." Jacob looked at me. "I couldn't do it." He turned away. "My dad did the first; its head upside down, poking out of the kill cone. He grabbed the head, pulled taught, cut its neck, and stood back as the blood streamed to the ground. About ten seconds later the bird stopped shaking. Dead."

Jacob looked back at me and I *could* read his mind this time; knew what he was going to say, almost the exact words. "One second there's life," Jacob said. "And a second later it's gone. Now there's always killing going on at the farm, but this hit me different. They were my birds. I didn't give them names, but I knew them, their personalities. I grew them. I didn't want to kill them."

I remember that Jacob's father was a no-frills guy. He spoke very few words, and then only after giving them a lot of consideration. Once when I was visiting Jacob, I asked his father how he was doing: one of those courtesy questions you ask out of duty to make some contact, check the box, before you ignore the person. His father took off his cap, looked up for a long moment, he stared down at his boots, his gaze went off to the distance, over the top of his barn, and then he turned to me, made severe eye contact, and said, "Pretty well."

"I reasoned with my dad that we could use them for eggs," Jacob said. "He agreed I could give it a try." Jacob looked at the bottle, as though the memory was swimming in there. "He agreed way too quick."

Lina and I never had kids. We wanted them, but none ever came. As time went on we thought this was a blessing: the farm was a lot of work, and money was always tight. We didn't want to be the generation that lost the farm, and we had no interest in passing the weight of it all to another. Lina took an hourly job at the local grocery store. It was a big chain, good benefits, some discounts. Employees could take home those unsold, precooked chickens, and everything in the deli that wouldn't keep overnight. The store was open 24/7, even Thanksgiving, and Christmas.

Between Lina's shift work and me living with the cows and fields, we'd become roommates. The only physical contact I had with anyone anymore was on the track.

"I was happy," Jacob said. "At first." He reached into his pocket and popped what I thought were little mints into his mouth. "But the birds kept growing. Two weeks later their legs couldn't support their massive bodies. Some broke their legs trying to walk. They'd sit there in their own shit, unable to move. I had to bring food and water right to them." Jacob swallowed another mint. "I could tell they were getting sick, brown green goo coming from their noses and eyes, sneezing all the time. After another week they started to die."

We had a cancer scare with Lina: a lump in her breast. It turned out to be nothing serious. The goddamn wait was what got to me; the time between the biopsy and the results. Five days. Without her salary, I knew if she died I'd lose the farm in a month or two. When that settled in, I felt guilty: I had a sense of relief. It wouldn't be my fault. I'd probably just walk away from the property, the equipment, and the endless debt. Finally free. The farm required more attention than newborn triplets; I couldn't remember the last time Lina and I were able to get away, even for a weekend. I forgot what it was like to be untethered from work, I wondered if I could even survive that kind of freedom.

"I told my dad he was right," Jacob said. "Should have killed them." There was a sharpness to Jacob's speech. After all that booze, no slurred words. Maybe he was an alcoholic? I never took him as one, just a good old boy, a heavy weekend drinker. "I asked my dad to help me kill them. End their misery. My dad just shook his head, and told me no, you watch them die, and you never question me again when it comes to animals." Jacob spit out the car window. "Within three weeks, they were all gone. Could have only had ten seconds of pain, their meat used to nourish others; instead, they had weeks of agony; disgusting, smelly carcasses that we had to burn." He took another mint. "Because of me."

I never told Lina about the upcoming foreclosure. I handled all the money; prided myself on keeping the banks at arm's length; now we were nose to nose. It could be a blessing to lose the farm; start somewhere fresh, but it's like my denim jacket with the broken zipper, frustrating every time I put it on; but gotta keep it; finding a new one that fits just right would be too much work.

"My insurance," Jacob said, "would pay off a lot of debt: enough for my place…and another." He tipped up his head and sniffed. "Smells like rain." He looked at me. "I bought a drone, an expensive one with a camera to look over my fields. Where to irrigate, fertilize." He looked out the window, away from me. "It's too much, the thought of being the one to lose the farm. The *Charming Poly*, the trek to Wisconsin, laid to waste by me." He looked back, and put his hand on my shoulder. I want to go home now to sleep. "I've been saving these up for a year." He showed me the bottle of mints. I saw a T-something on the label. Jacob popped a few more into his mouth. "Took the drone up today to see where those bastards damaged your field. Funny, I couldn't see a single tire track, just that hole twenty yards ahead of us." He curled up on the seat like a tired dog. "You don't have it thought through. Don't do something stupid. I've got it figured out. Take me home, get me to bed."

Jacob started to snore. I drove the car to the field's edge, sat and thought. The Impala made a ticking sound, probably a bad piston, or rod, or both. Upwards of $1,500 to fix, more money I didn't have.

If I went left, a few miles down the road was Jacob's house. A right turn, and a fifteen-minute drive, would get us to the emergency entrance of St. Elisabeth's hospital.

The summer breeze had turned into a wind; a storm *was* on the way. Above the car engine sputter, the cornrows still crackled like fire, once distant, but now, closer.

I pulled onto the road. I thought about those chickens.

A Different Position

I decided to cut my toenails. Carol, my wife, made the suggestion. We were reading in the living room. My bare feet were propped up on a coffee table. "Your feet are disgusting," she said. "Cut your toenails. No wonder all your socks have holes in them and our bed sheets are getting torn up."

I understood the sock issue. That's why I buy them in ten-packs from Walmart: gray, low-cut athletic socks for everyday use, and black mid-calf dress socks for work. Carol does the laundry and she throws out the socks with holes in the toes. Eventually, there aren't two socks left to pair. Then I buy a new batch.

The bed sheets took me longer to figure out. It wasn't the bed sheets. It was the bed pad cover. There were two spots near the bottom that were scraped, the fabric showed signs of wear, as though a dog had dug for a bone. The locations of the two areas are exactly where my feet are planted when we make love or have sex. In the past, we were more creative, but after twenty years of marriage, we settled on the missionary position. I am always the one to initiate sex. I imagined my feet digging, toes curling when I was close to orgasm; hence the holes.

I sat on the closed toilet in the bathroom, clipper in hand, and studied my feet. The big toes, dark from persistent fungal infections, looked like the tips of battle-weary, medieval weapons. The three middle toenails had irregular shapes, curling out in different directions. The little toe was not really a nail, just an extended nub.

I started on my big toe, and the clipper broke, separating into two pieces. The silver implement was useless now. A loose piece of toenail jutted out, still attached. I peeled it off. Blood seeped around the edge of the nail plate to the cuticle. The nail was left with a sharp edge. Perhaps I could smooth it with the Dremel in the toolshed. Carol drove up. I dabbed the blood with a piece of toilet paper, put on my socks, and went down to greet her.

Carol worked long hours. She is a logistics manager, responsible for shipping new product launches, which happen every two months. She led a team of seven. I'm always hesitant to ask her how her day went. The answer is never good, or okay: she is always dealing with a crisis. I asked.

"Horrible," Carol said. "We have a new launch, the new adult incontinence pants, and we are going to miss getting the product to our top five customers by a week."

"I'm sorry honey," I said. From the tone in her voice I could tell this was not the usual crisis.

"It's all my fault," she said. "I really screwed up some calculations."

"Does a week make that much difference?" I said. "Just sell the old diapers until the new ones arrive."

She launched into a monologue, not talking to me at all. "We shifted production to the new pants, let the old inventory run down. We have nothing to fill the shelves with: we'll lose shelf space. A competitor will step in and we'll never get it back." She put her hand to her mouth, looked up, pulled her hand away, and exhaled smoke from an imaginary cigarette. "We have national ads running, a social media blitz. We'll lose our endcaps, we'll have to throw away millions in displays. This will hit our margins: they'll be shit for years." Carol looked at me, her eyes now focused. "I'm going to get fired."

"Carol," I said, "it's just diapers."

"Aren't you listening to me?" she said. "I. Am. Going. To. Get. Fired." She leaned toward me. "Stop calling them diapers. They're adult incontinence pants. *Fucking pants.*"

I thought: *diapers, fucking diapers*, and hoped I didn't say it out loud.

After a dinner of leftover meatloaf and mashed potatoes, I reminded Carol that I had the next day off from school. I would catch up on my work.

"I might leave you a short list, if that's OK?" I nodded.

While Carol was on her laptop and phone, I went up to bed and fell asleep grading papers. I wished I taught high school math, instead of English. The grading process would be much more objective. Binary: correct or incorrect. Perhaps grammar tests are more straightforward, but that night it was creative writing. I circled spelling issues, added commas, removed commas, drew arrows to teach attribution variety, red ticks to point out tense issues, vague pronouns, subject-verb agreement errors, and run-on sentences. It was as though I was looking at software: I rarely commented on story.

Teaching is an honorable profession, but my MFA was meant to birth me as a writer. Work on my novel, a few substitute teaching gigs for a little cash. But a full-time offer came, with benefits, a pension; how could I say no? I'd write at night, take the summers off to hit the keyboard round-the-clock. Then I picked up summer classes.

"What do you do?" they'd ask.

"I'm a writer." How exciting, they would say. I would talk and talk, until my wife kicked me under the table, alerting me that everyone's eyes had glassed over and I hadn't noticed.

"What do you do?" they'd ask.

"I am an English teacher." Oh, they would say, the wine is nice huh?

My novel, *The Terbium Dominion*, was about a group of people in a small Midwestern town, with superpowers of X-ray vision, the result of their drinking water being polluted by fracking. Ninety pages of the book are in the bottom right-hand drawer of my desk at home. I'll never finish it.

The next morning, papers were scattered on my lap and the floor. The reading lamp was still on. Carol never came to bed. I assumed she went back to work; pulled an all-nighter. This was not unusual behavior for her in crisis mode. This was much better for me than to have her tossing and turning in bed all night. She was not one to sit around and worry when she could get to work on the issue.

A note on the kitchen cutting board only had one item: vacuum the living room. I already knew when I reported to her that I completed the task she would ask: did you do under the cushions?

I ran our canister vacuum cleaner over the hardwood floor, the center carpet, and under the tables. I pulled the pillows off of our new, L-shaped sectional couch, and threw them in a pile on the floor. Why we needed eight pillows, I will never know. Two or three could make sense, but not eight. Then, I grabbed each of the six bottom cushions; six back cushions, and tossed them with the pillows. Underneath, I found remnants from my late-night snacks: popcorn, granola, and the occasional coin. I saw a quarter and picked it up. It was one of my lucky coins, the one I used at the coffee break flips at work.

The other teachers and I would gather in the private lounge each day at ten-fifteen and perform a ritual to see who was going to pay for coffee each day. For safety reasons we had to remove the coffee maker from the lounge, forcing us to buy crap coffee in the cafeteria. Seven or eight of us would form a circle. We would agree on either heads or tails and then flip. If heads was selected, everyone with heads was out. The remaining group who had flipped tails would flip again. This would continue until only one person was left. That teacher would have to buy the coffee. At a buck a cup it would run seven or eight dollars. I rarely lost. My coworkers always commented on my persistent fortune. They did not know about my lucky coins.

A number of months ago, I lost the flip four days in a row. I went home and created my lucky coins. Using super glue, I made two two-headed coins: one tails and one heads. Each day when we decided what side was the winner, I would use that coin, always keeping the heads coin in my left pocket and the tails coin in my right.

The idea came from my grandfather. He had a two-headed quarter he used as an icebreaker at the bar where he tended. Grandpa Marco was second generation from Italy. A well-respected man; a gentleman who picked imaginary pieces of lint off the shoulders of patrons; ready to help a family member or friend any time of the day or night, and a hell of a golfer. When he was a kid, he was a badass. My mother told me story after story of him skipping grade school to caddy at the public course; he would hop trains as a teenager, disappear across the country for weeks on end.

Just dropping it all to wander the land: a luxury for simpler times. These days that urge to just go was a persistent demon on my shoulder; more than a lottery-winning fantasy: brown Bullboxer Brosus boots, a well-worn, open-road cowboy hat, duckwork carpenter pants, a white shirt and suspenders, a little cash, a manual typewriter, the rumble of the tracks under my feet, wind burning my cheeks; nowhere to go but forward into the unknown, to adventure.

The double-sided coins worked. At first, after a few days, I was going to reveal my trick coins, let everyone in on the joke. But the longer I went on winning, the harder it was for me to make the admission. After three weeks it was less of a practical joke and more of a crime. I remembered reading when the Allies broke the Enigma code machine in WWII, they would have to ignore information they received now and then, so as not to let the Germans know they broke the code. Perhaps let a shipment of weapons pass, or turn a blind eye to an attack on the fleet. I imagined how difficult it must have been to have the knowledge to prevent an attack, yet allow people to be killed: a sacrifice for a greater good.

To avoid suspicion, and quell my guilt with the coin flip cheats, I'd force a loss now and then, but at a much less frequency than if I left it up to chance. I was never a very lucky person in life unless I cheated: dealing from the bottom of the card deck in high school, buying answers to history exams in college, padding charitable donations on my taxes, a two-headed coin. Everyone cheats.

The stack of cushions and pillows piled on the floor made me think of Devil's Tower: a bucket list trip. My GPS said it was thirteen hours and thirty-nine minutes away. If I left now, just went straight West, I could be there just at sunset.

After thoroughly vacuuming the couch: down the cracks; run the Dyson's floor nozzle over each cushion; I thought *tails*. The coin flicked off my left thumb, caught by my right hand and slapped down on the back of my left hand. Tails.

I decided to go.

During the drive I wondered what Carol would think when I returned. When would I get the first phone call: *Where the hell are you? I'm worried sick!* I could not think of a good explanation, nothing that would make any sense to her, or me. So I put that aside and drove. Listened to the Grateful Dead on satellite radio. *Truckin' got my chips cashed in. Keep truckin', like the do-dah man. Together, more or less in line, just keep truckin' on.* The music put me at ease; dissolved me into something bigger than myself.

After four hours I pulled off the highway and drove for two miles until I came across a small gas station. The sign at the entrance said *Hank's*.

A note was taped to the pump. Scraggy letters printed with a sharpie stated, "Fill up first then pay inside." It was that kind of small town. The pump's bell dinged at each dollar; a series of numbers rolled by on three tumblers. Retro, but here it was authentic.

More bells rang above me when I opened the door to the station. The aisles in the small shop were crammed full of beer, hard liquor, candy, canned goods, car supplies, and work clothes. On my way to the counter, I passed a rack stuffed with gun and fishing magazines.

Behind the counter stood a big man, old, military-short gray hair. He wore a blue long-sleeved button work shirt, wide red suspenders, his ample gut hanging over his pants. "Hank" was embroidered over the shirt's pocket. Next to him, a young guy sat on a stool reading something on an iPad; his dirty blond hair pulled into a ponytail.

I missed the days when everyone read actual books. It was a hobby of mine, sitting on an airplane, a hospital waiting room, the DMV, observing what people read; a glimpse into who they were: the guy in a suit reading a Grisham novel, the old lady consumed in Proust, the hipster kid reading Kerouac, the young woman with a shaved head studying the Bhagavad-Gita.

"What can I do for you," Hank said.

"The gas, and a large coffee," I said.

"How much you get?" I realized he had no way of knowing.

"Thirty-four dollars." I topped off the tank at that exact number.

He nodded. "The coffee will be a buck." I handed him a credit card.

"Sorry." Hank shook his big head. "We only take cash." He frowned. "Is that a problem?"

"No." I handed him two twenties. "That's easy," I said.

Hank grinned. "Easy as a drunk girl on prom night." I winced. "Coffee's in the back. I'll make a fresh pot."

"Oh, that's alright," I said. We can skip the coffee."

"Come on now son," Hank said. "I offered to make it for you. I always make a fresh pot this time of day. What's your rush?"

"Sure," I said. The bells above the door rang. A woman walked in. She was around about forty. Her black overcoat seemed too much for the heat of the day. She moved a white cane back and forth as she made her way to the counter. Her oversized sunglasses were the type a doctor gave you after having your pupils dilated.

The kid looked up from his iPad.

"Afternoon, Beth," Hank said. "The usual?"

"Yes," she said in almost a whisper. "One cream and three sugars." Hank nodded and disappeared into the back. My bills sat on the counter.

She was very attractive: straight, shoulder-length black hair, fit; even with the bulky coat I could tell she had large breasts. The kid reached down and retrieved something from his backpack; looked over his shoulder, and slid a small package, tightly wrapped in brown paper toward Beth. She handed him some bills and quickly put the package into her coat pocket. No words were exchanged.

She looked at me. "What do you want to know?" she said.

"So you're…"

"Blind," she said. "From birth." I was going to ask her where she was from.

"Not many blind folks around here," she said. "You don't see them out and about." I realized this was accurate. I couldn't remember seeing a blind person, in years. Why was this? Modern medical advances eradicating the issue? Cocooned up at home with technology that enabled them to stay at home, productive, entertained; safe from a bustling world.

"Do you dream?" I said. The question surprised me.

"Yes," she said. "The same as you, but with no sight. Bodily sensations. Psychological conflicts. I feel, smell, touch, taste, have the fear of missing a final exam, panic at my teeth falling out, delight in flying…fucking."

My eyes were drawn to the mystery of what was under that coat.

Hank came back and set down two coffees: Styrofoam cups, flimsy plastic tops. Beth slid a dollar across the counter. Hank took it; more bells rang on the old, oversized cash register. He slammed the cash drawer shut.

"Could I also have a pack of cigarettes?" I said.

"Sure," Hank said. "What's your poison?"

"American Spirits," I said. "Bright yellow."

He turned, scanned the shelf, and retrieved the pack. He turned the pack over in his hand. Examined it. "What are these?" he said. "Banana flavored?"

"I wish they were cheesesteak flavored," I said. "Maybe I'd lose some weight."

The kid perked up. "What if they were? People might start losing too much weight and the cigarette companies would have to add caloric content. Then chain smokers would gain too much weight, and they'd have to create low-fat cigarettes. The possibilities are endless."

Hank shook his head. "Sorry," he said. "Jimmy here wants to be a writer."

I thought about all those ungraded papers.

Hank turned the pack over in his hand. "Five bucks," he said.

"You sure," I said. "Is that enough?"

"Yep," Hank said. "But you can pay more if you want." He laughed and picked up the twenties. "This'll cover it."

"I've tried to quit," I said. "But it's hard."

Hank turned to the register. "Hard as a young groom's pecker on his honeymoon night." He rang it up, more bells, and he slammed the drawer.

"I wonder if you can give me some directions?" I said.

"Don't you have a…" Hank held an imaginary phone in his hand and searched for the word.

"A GPS? I do, but I'm heading west; looking for a more scenic route."

"Sure," Hank said. "Take a left out of the parking lot. Pass the highway entrance ramp and keep left. Then in a mile bear right; just past where the old schoolhouse used to be. It's a rustic road. Nice drive; through the park; along the edge of Miller's dairy farm. Nice view of Bethany Lake. The wife and I take that drive sometimes after Sunday church." He hitched a thumb under his suspender. "Where you headed to?"

"Not sure," I said. I didn't want to get into it.

"You gotta be going somewhere," Hank said.

"I'm not sure," I said.

Beth reached out and gently grabbed my arm. "Go back," she said. Through the dark glasses, she was looking right into my eyes. "If you're not sure where you're going, go back." I wondered what was in the package the kid gave her.

The bells jingled when I opened the door. I turned before exiting. The three of them watched me. Hank's hand gave me a short wave goodbye. I glanced at my watch and knew that if Carol worked late I still had a chance of beating her home.

I opened the cigarettes and gave them a sniff; it wasn't bananas, it was raisins. Something I never noticed before. The impact of the aroma was the opposite of on-the-road coffee, which always smelled great but tasted tolerable, like a hangover breakfast of flat beer and cold pizza. That first cigarette would be smooth, regulating my breath, a guided meditation. I threw the full pack into the beat-up, metal trashcan by the door, got into my car, and headed home.

The coffee was quite good.

At nine o'clock, I entered the driveway. Carol pulled in right behind me. We parked in the garage and got out of our cars.

Carol got out, slammed the car door, and rushed into the house. I knew I was in trouble. My mind went on an expedition for excuses.

When I entered the kitchen, Carol was over the sink. She filled a glass with water. Drank it. Then drank another. Filled it again, and drank about half. She turned to me. "Sorry, I was really thirsty. Where were you?"

"Got some gas." It wasn't a lie.

"We did it," she said. "That kid from MIT. The one everybody said would be a mistake for me to hire." Her hands were animated. Water from the glass sloshed onto the floor. "He filled the whiteboard with equations and figured it out. Truncated backhauls with double drops, engage the customer freight brokers, back off on a few replenishment loops. Everything's going to arrive on time."

"Congratulations," I said. "So you live to fight another battle."

She straightened. A dark stain the shape of Florida stood out, just below her chin. "Brandford, that asshole marketing VP, actually gave me a hug. Said I should get a promotion, head all the product departments." She was slurring her words.

"We had a few drinks afterward," she said.

"No shit," I said.

"One of the girls had pot," she said. "Medical marijuana. We took a few hits by the dumpsters behind the bar before going in. It's strong, not like the stuff we smoked in college. Just two hits and you are buzzed. More than buzzed."

"Huh," I said.

"I just had a few beers, and shots." She finished the water and set down the glass. "Jägermeister. Black stuff. Tastes like shit." She looked at me with a mischievous smile. "How do you put up with me? I swear you're a goddamned angel."

I asked her if she wanted something to eat.

"Let's go upstairs," she said, grabbed my arm, gave me a sloppy, tongue-filled kiss, and took me to the bedroom.

Our clothes and my ungraded papers were scattered on the floor. I was on top of her. She squeezed my ass cheeks, with each thrust, pulled me in deep. Her eyes were shut. She moaned. The bed frame banged against the wall.

I stopped.

"What's wrong?" she said, the words exhaled.

"The sheets," I said. "My toenails."

Carol laughed, messed my hair with her hands, propped herself up, kissed my forehead, pushed me off, grabbed my shoulders, planted me on my back, and got on top.

The world compressed into friction and sweat.

We were heading somewhere; I'm not sure of the destination.

It didn't matter.

The Death of God

It knew itself as awareness. No center. No end. Awareness. It did not know its name. It had no I. A perturbation arose - from where? The agitation expanded—a significant change. It grew. It caused disruption—a point of focus with hope for discovery—all new concepts for it. It asked why. It hoped it would speak its name.

SCIENTISTS DECIDED THAT the universe was billions of years old. From the pinprick of the Big Bang, it was expanding in all directions at the speed of light. Intelligence, as measured through the development of languages (approximated at seven thousand) was starting to disappear. But as the dialects of man dwindled, with increased attention to the universal tongue of mathematics, the languages of animals were discovered and categorized: the song of whales, the chirps of birds, the movements of bees, the barking patterns of dogs. Beyond these, the languages of what were once thought to be unintelligent objects made themselves evident.

Aspen trees with their interconnected root systems, and ability to sway in the wind, which freed microscopic cells to be carried through the air to others of its type, were found to send messages of drought and fire over hundreds of miles.

Mycelium roots were determined to be the largest living organisms, connecting and communicating over thousands of miles.

The movement of the wind and seas, thought to be the results of physical phenomena, such as changes in atmospheric pressures and the gravitational pull of the moon, were discovered to be complex dialects, with messages that gave rise to the climate transitions on the earth. The oceans, the large lakes, and the small trickling streams carried their messages across the earth: water evaporated, molecules transmitted their utterances through the sky, and the wind moved these codes, depositing information, to receptors, with rain.

The name of a god was thought to hold a final power; to know a god was to speak its name. Christ. Allah. Shiva. Vishnu. Elohim. Elah. Shangdi. Maykapal. Bhragava. Surendra. To know this name was man's purpose for existence; its discovery, spoken aloud, as a prayer, would bring the purpose of man's existence to an end.

Hebrew intellects searched the ancient texts for the all-encompassing name of God. The many representations all had their purpose. The Tetragrammaton YHWH: Yahweh: Jehovah, a piece, yet incomplete. The art of Kabbalah wedded with mathematics to divine the name. But it was the final discovery that gave the greatest hope.

Geologists agreed that the most inanimate of objects were alive—and had language. Stones spoke. The earth's land-masses, once a single unit, had split into continents: separate parts that yearned to be whole. The 500,000 detectable earthquakes every year began to shape into an alphabet. Many, perceived by only the most sensitive scientific instruments, were seen as a constant chatter: words, sentences, and paragraphs. The largest destructive quakes were theorized to be shouts of pain, calling to their distant pieces. The religion of Gaia: a sentient earth, characterized these as soulful cries of longing across the chasms—lost love.

The earth went silent. As decades progressed with no quakes, the geo-linguists (a science to some, a religion to others), developed more precise instruments and found the mountains themselves spoke. The utterance of a single syllable took years. A word—centuries. The meshing of science and religion turned from the subatomic world for answers, to the macro, the large, the most visible of physical entities. It gave man hope that in the study of these ancient beings, the purpose of creation had focus, and struggled to speak the name of God.

Society, with its diverse economies, competing philosophies, anxious religions, and growing technologies, served to further divide man, rather than make them whole. Peace was always torn at its fundamental fabric by war. Love was subdued by hate.

When the sun grew in size by 20% (a surprise event that would reshape the theories of astrophysicists—if there were any to see it), all organic life on the earth was destroyed—in an instant.

The rocks continued to talk, for thousands of years, in the quiet of a dissolved humanity and moved toward the first utterance of God's name. When the sun expanded again, the earth was gone, vaporized—its quarks, fermions, and leptons, were pulled apart, separated forever, blown in all directions to chaos, to nothingness.

IT SENSED THE LOSS. It asked why. It wondered if it had a name. It became as it was before. It knew itself as awareness. No center. No end.

Never Stop Exiting

It's around ten at night in Kyoto, the Cherry Blossom Festival is in full swing. After spending the day walking the Philosophers Path, we headed to Maruyama Park. There is a chill in the air and we are not dressed for it. The guy working the food stand hands me two cups of warm sake. "I'm sorry I only ordered fries."

"No, free for you; you writer. Hemingway, drink right?"

I nodded and took the drinks. "This is beautiful," I said pointing to all the illuminated trees.

"It will all be gone tomorrow," he said. "Rainstorm and wind, all blossoms will come down."

"That's sad," I said.

"Not sad," he said. "Nothing is permanent and this reminds us. But look now and enjoy. It all gone tomorrow. Just like life. That's why we celebrate now, to remember this. To enjoy this now." He smiled at me.

I bump into a girl. Her t-shirt says "Never Stop Exiting." I'm in Kyoto, away from our home in Osaka, away from home in Korea, which is away from home in Wisconsin.

I'm nervous about how late it is, and still having to navigate the cab, and bus, and subway, to get back to Osaka. But the trees are gorgeous—iridescent. The crowd is alive and happy. The sake is warm. My girlfriend of forty-two years is smiling. I do not care about anything but now.

Acknowledgments

Gratefully acknowledged are the following publicaitons, were certain stories appeared in earlier versions:

"The Tallest Mountain in the World" in *Coolest American Stories 2022*

"Static" in *Wisconsin People & Ideas*; "Static" received first place in the 2018 *Wisconsin People & Ideas* Fiction Contest and Honorable Mention in the March/April 2017 Glimmer Train Fiction Open.

"Full Count" in *Pleiades*

"The French Paperclip," "The Blue Blazer," "Frank's Used Books," and "The Samadhi Tones" in *Moss Piglet*

"The Death of God" in *365tomorrows*

There is a legion of people who have supported my writing career. A special thanks to my primary writing mentor, and good friend, Steven Polansky, I'd be nowhere without your patience and guidance. When I edit my stories it's your voice I hear in my head giving me advice.

Several editors worked with me to improve and publish my fiction, making me a better writer. Thank you to: Jason

Smith, Phong Nguyen, John Bloner, Mark Wish, Elizabeth Coffey, Stephen Smith, and Kenneth James Crist.

I was also fortunate to have many fellow writers generously give me their time for advice and encouragement: Abby Frucht, Jim Knipfel, Charles Johnson, Steve Fox, Nikki Kallio, Nickolas Butler, Karla Houston, Deauwand Meyers, Richie Zaborowske, and Adam Levine.

Thank you to Judy Bauerlein and Eric Rolland for bringing my first published story "Static" to the big screen.

My early days as a book and music critic helped me hone some of the skills I apply to fiction. Thank you to Derek Davis, Peter Stone Brown, Dan Deluca, Tom Moon, Linda Hasert, Tom Breuer, Joe Amann, Eric T. Miller, and Geeta Jensen.

My sons are a constant source of inspiration. Thank you Michael, Nathan, and Garrett. I'm proud of the men you've become.

Thank you to my parents, for bringing me into the world, and encouraging me to be curious about life.

To the great, energetic team at Cornerstone Press: publisher Dr. Ross Tangedal, editorial director Brett Hill and his team, Paige Biever for the cover design, and Sophie McPherson, Ava Willett, Autumn Vine, and Madison Schultz in media and sales.

To my muse, my travel companion, my wife, Heidi, thank you for always being there for me in the past, and for the many adventures that lay on the long road ahead of us.

Michael Hopkins was born in Philadelphia, Pennsylvania. His book and music criticism has appeared in the *Philadelphia Inquirer, Philadelphia Weekly, Milwaukee Journal Sentinel, The Scene* (WI), and *Magnet.* He has a degree in electrical engineering from Drexel University. His stories have won awards from *Glimmer Train* and The Mill. His short fiction has been published in *Coolest American Stories 2022, Millwork, Pleiades, 365 Tomorrows, Wisconsin People and Ideas, Black Petals,* and *Moss Piglet.* He is the winner of the 2018 Wisconsin Academy of Science, Arts and Letters annual fiction contest, and 3rd place winner in the 2019 contest. He lives on a hobby farm in Wisconsin, with his wife and their dog, cats, chickens, and bees.

For more information, visit michaelhopkinswriter.com.

www.ingramcontent.com/pod-product-compliance
Lightning Source LLC
Chambersburg PA
CBHW031050310726
48969CB00007B/2198